TOM MALONE

American Snapshots

This book was professionally typeset on Reedsy.
Find out more at reedsy.com

For Delaney and Isaiah

"Photography takes an instant out of time, altering life by holding it still."

- Dorothea Lange

Preface

A country tends to focus on a common narrative, a singular story that aims to unify us all under one umbrella. This common story often projects images of positivity and possibility, well-intentioned to bring people together.

But, so often, the individual citizens of a country don't see their lives reflected in this singular plotline. Their lives diverge from the narrative.

The fact is that a country is too grand in scope to fit within the confines of one common story. A country is so much more than that.

The story of a country is defined by its people. And people have their own stories, their own narratives, their own plotlines. A person's life doesn't have the same highs and lows as the person next door, nor does a person's story fit the same timeline as a person two states over. Some people's stories express themes of joy and triumph, while others elicit feelings of sadness and anger.

Everyone's story is different.

Everyone's story is valid.

The story of a country doesn't exist in isolation. We are all a product of what came before us, tethered to our ancestors and their actions in ways that we may never understand.

The story of a country is segmented by region; each region, formed by its people and its history, create subcultures and

i

subhistories that further write the stories of those who were born into them.

The story of a country is always changing, always evolving with new people, new actions, new thoughts. What was true yesterday might not matter today. What matters today might drastically impact the plot of tomorrow.

The story of a country is anything but singular. It is a collection of snapshots layered on top of and beside one another, forming a more complete picture of the whole story. Each layer reveals another element to the complex interconnectivity of the story being told.

The story of a country is never complete. No matter how many perspectives and accounts and lenses we use, we can never fully grasp the entire plot, nor can we experience every character.

But that's part of the allure of a country's story. The more we understand, the more elusive it becomes.

All we can do is tell the story the best we can.

Here is one such attempt.

This is the story of a country.

The Truck

Thick air clung to Matt's clothes. He couldn't decide if he was sweating, or if the air was that humid. Sun dipped below the horizon, coating the evening with vibrant hues of orange and pink. Dew dropped from Matt's glass of sweet tea. A ring formed on the old table.

The woods around the house were quiet. Matt enjoyed the quiet sometime. It provided him with an opportunity to think, to reflect.

But tonight, he would have enjoyed some noise. A break from his over-analytical mind. He just wanted to let loose at the party like everyone else. Like a soon-to-be junior in high school was supposed to.

Junior year. A rite of passage. At least it was supposed to be. It was supposed to indicate a rise to the top of the social pyramid. But that's not how things were playing out.

And summer seemed to be slipping away.

A rusty truck rumbled toward the house. Dust clouded the long dirt driveway, obstructing Matt's view. But he already knew who it was.

The truck crawled to the front porch and creaked to a stop.

Joshua hopped out and slammed his door.

"Come on, man," Joshua said. "Just come to the party."

Matt rolled his eyes.

"You know I can't go," Matt said.

He wanted to go. He *really* wanted to go.

"I know you *say* you can't go," Joshua said, "but I think you're just making excuses."

"I am not," Matt said. "My mom won't let me."

A mischievous spark flashed across Joshua's eyes.

"Just tell Ms. Lottie that you're staying at my house tonight," Joshua said. "You know, to celebrate my cousin's birthday or something."

"*Lie* to my mother?" Matt said. "You've got to be crazy."

Joshua smirked. The idea seemed to have moved away from him for now.

"Alright man," Joshua said. "If you change your mind, let me know. And I hope you change your mind."

Matt high-fived Joshua, his dark skin contrasting with Joshua's pale hand.

Dust kicked up as Joshua's truck sped down the dirt road. Matt sat on the steps of his porch. He watched as the last flickers of twilight hung in the darkening sky.

He wanted to go to the party. He *really* wanted to go to the party. That's what junior year was supposed to be all about.

Then again, all the rich kids from the North Side of town would be there. It's not that Matt didn't like the North Siders. They were probably nice enough. He just didn't go into that part of town much. It gave him an uneasy feeling. People from the North Side just had a different way of doing things, from what Matt could see.

But Amaya would probably be there. She was technically a

North Sider, but she had roots in Matt's part of town. And she acted like a South Sider. Laid back, genuine, fun, grounded.

Yeah. Amaya would be there. Matt didn't mind that Amaya probably didn't know who he was. But she could find out tonight at the party.

Matt grabbed his cup of sweet tea and finished it. He knew what he had to do.

* * *

Music vibrated from somewhere in the woods. As Matt walked closer, he saw lights glisten through the trees. Then, the loud chatter of high schoolers began to echo. He kept walking until the trees opened into a clearing.

This is beautiful, Matt thought. *My first real high school party*.

It was just like the movies he had seen. Old trucks lined the clearing, tailgates open. Speakers pumped music through the crowd. Small groups gathered and talked while free-spirits danced in the center. Football players in letterman jackets patrolled the party, while wandering eyes followed their paths.

But something seemed off.

His suspicions had proven accurate.

As Matt stood back and watched, he started to notice that no one from his side of town was at the party. The party was full of North Siders.

Even though everyone in town all went to the same high school, the divide was palpable.

Suddenly, Matt felt displaced. He looked around for Joshua, the only North Sider who treated Matt like an equal.

Matt looked through the darkness. He thought he spotted Joshua's rusty truck on the other side of the clearing, but it was difficult to distinguish among so many other old trucks. He grabbed his plastic sweet tea bottle and walked into the crowd. As Matt weaved between people, he squinted his eyes, trying to see if it was really Joshua who sat on the rusty truck's tailgate.

"Matt?" a voice called from the crowd.

"Amaya," Matt said. "What's up?"

Amaya smiled. Her eyes creased.

"I didn't know you were coming to the party tonight," Amaya said. "I usually don't see you at these things."

Matt shifted on his feet. She *did* know who he was. He wanted to take a drink of sweet tea to calm himself down. It might give him time to think of a clever reply. He twisted the lid, but then decided against it. He didn't want to spill on himself, or cough, or something embarrassing. So he just held the plastic bottle.

"I'm not much of a partier," Matt said.

"That's alright," Amaya said. "To be honest, neither am I. Actually, I've only been to one other party."

A new song blared through the speakers. Matt opened his mouth to say something, but two girls approached Amaya and pulled her toward the dancing crowd.

"See you later," Amaya said.

Matt waved with the bottle in his hand. He continued his path through the crowd until he neared the rusty truck.

"Matt!" Joshua shouted from inside the truck bed.

Joshua waved Matt toward the truck. A few unfamiliar faces stood around the truck. One waved awkwardly, a motion that Matt returned.

"Is this that dude you've told us about?" a North Sider asked Joshua.

Joshua nodded. They both suppressed a laugh.

"I didn't think you'd show up," Joshua continued. "Ms. Lottie let you out of the house, huh?"

"No, not exactly," Matt said. "I told her I was going to your house."

That wasn't true. Matt had simply asked his mother. She allowed him to go under two conditions: he would return home by ten o'clock and he had better not drink. However, Matt knew that a story like this could give him some credentials, masking his lack of party experience. Joshua raised his hands above his head, revealing the beer can in his hand.

"I'm glad you finally listened to me," Joshua said.

He looked around to his friends for nods of affirmation.

"Well, man," Joshua said, "you want a drink?"

Matt had been afraid of this question. He didn't want to drink a beer. But he saw all the kids in the movies doing it at high school parties. He shifted on his feet.

"No, thanks," Matt said. "I brought my own."

"No way!" Joshua shouted. "What did you spike it with?"

Matt smiled. He felt his face flush.

"Just sweet tea," Matt said.

He held up his sweet tea bottle. One of Joshua's friends snickered. Joshua acknowledged the laugh with a smirk.

Matt's temperature rose. He felt embarrassed at his admission. But that embarrassment turned to suppressed anger. Joshua was never demeaning toward Matt. That wasn't how their friendship operated.

"I didn't know you were such a wimp," Joshua said. "Just have a beer, man."

Matt squinted his eyes. He cocked his head to one side as he looked at Joshua, and then his eyes drifted to the North Siders.

"No, Josh," Matt said. "I'm good. I'm just here to post up and see what these parties in the woods are all about."

"You do you," Joshua said.

He leaned back against the truck and returned his attention to his North Side friends. Matt felt the group begin to close him out.

"Alright, Josh," Matt said. "I'll see you later. I'm going to go check in with some people."

Joshua threw his hand up in recognition and continued his conversation with a North Side friend. Matt stepped away from the truck and merged into the crowd again with no destination in mind. He felt lost, adrift in a sea of unfamiliar faces. He wished his sweet tea had something else in it.

"Matt!" Amaya shouted.

She dodged a few people dancing and stood in front of Matt.

"Sorry my friends cut us off," Amaya said. "They loved that song."

"No worries," Matt said. "Do you like to dance?"

Amaya smiled. Matt felt his embarrassment and fear drain from his face. Somehow, the need to impress dissipated.

"I love to dance," Amaya said. "And I love this song."

Matt looked into her eyes. She knew who he was.

"Do you want to dance?"

The Axe

Alaska

Summer and pollen hung in the air. The scent of pine tree sap and distant salt water floated on a breeze that still carried remnants of an arctic winter. It was late in the evening, but sunlight streaked the sky, deceptive in its indication of time.

Everyone in the house was already asleep, but the sunlight kept the girl awake. The girl zipped her jacket over her thick sweatshirt, a shield from the elements. She stepped outside and closed the door behind her, careful to twist the doorknob before the latch clicked shut and jolted her parents awake. She didn't want to be bothered with questions.

"Yikes, it's cold," the girl whispered.

The Alaskan wind evoked a sense of survival, even in the summer.

She walked across the grass. Some of it crunched beneath her feet and it seemed to echo through the woods. It had been an unusually dry summer.

The girl approached the wood pile, hundreds of rounded pieces of tree trunks stacked in a semi-organized heap. An old axe laid by a log, its blade glistening in the sunlight. She picked up a log and flipped it on its end. Picking up the axe, she eyed the center of the log's rings. She fixed her attention on the center of the circle. Lifting the axe above her head, she channeled all of her emotion into the blade. She pulled down with the entire force of her body.

"Bullseye," she said.

The dry log split in half, sending a crackle through the forest. Two halves fell on opposing sides.

"These should fit," the girl said.

Her house was old. Her grandfather built it a long time ago. The house was small, heated solely by a wood stove. People from other states would have viewed her house as a mountain cabin, quaint and isolated on the edge of town. But the girl just perceived it as home.

She set up another log, raised the axe, and chopped.

Chop. Crackle. Repeat.

The girl enjoyed chopping wood by herself. It allowed her to focus on one, solitary task. It allowed her to escape the pressures of middle school, the chaos of her siblings, and her anxiety about the future.

But, sometimes, those dreams of the future crept into her mind. Sometimes, she thought about growing up and getting out of this town. She didn't have a particular destination in mind. When she watched movies about adults, they all took place in big cities. Places like New York and Los Angeles. Maybe she'd move there and work at a coffee shop or something. Take taxis everywhere. Maybe the subway. Go out to dinner at trendy restaurants.

Just like the movies.

Chop. Crackle. Repeat.

When she got older, she'd get an apartment downtown somewhere. With a few friends, perhaps. She'd work in a big office in a tall building. A skyscraper, taller than Alaskan trees. The office would have wide windows so she could look out over the city. She'd buy new clothes sometimes, whatever the latest fashion trend was going to be. Bright colors. Hats. Shoes with heels.

Just like the movies.

Chop. Crackle. Repeat.

She'd listen to the street noise: cars honking, bicycles chiming, people shouting. She'd buy magazines from carts on the street corners. She'd order coffee drinks from baristas.

Just like the movies.

Chop. Crackle. Repeat.

She'd spend her nights on rooftops with friends, dancing the night away under the stars and city lights.

Just like the movies.

Chop. Crackle. Repeat.

The girl stopped chopping wood. She had heard a noise somewhere in the forest. She put the axe down slowly, silently. As she knelt down to the ground, she watched a moose walk cautiously through the woods.

The girl's heart thumped. Her breath quickened. But she forced herself to remain calm. Animals could sense danger and anxiety, so she refocused herself and extended safety.

"Hey there, buddy," the girl whispered.

The moose looked at her, trying to decipher the girl's motive.

"I'm not gonna hurt you," she said.

The moose seemed to decide that the girl was no threat, so it continued its stroll through the forest. Quiet, accustomed to the routines of the wilderness. The moose walked so peacefully. The only noise in the entire forest came from the soft steps of the moose as it inched its way from one tree to the next, following a path it had likely taken hundreds of time, methodical in its rugged routine.

Not like the movies.

Maybe the wilderness wasn't so bad. In fact, maybe the wilderness was the purest form of living. No artificial noise to disrupt the quiet. The hustle and bustle of city life had no purpose here.

The moose took one last look at the girl before moving onward through the forest. The girl waited until the moose had time to move forward in peace. She closed her eyes and listened to the silence. She allowed herself to smile.

Then, the girl lined up a log and picked up the axe.

Chop. Crackle. Repeat.

The Guitar

Steam rose from the tea kettle as it began its low whistle. Mariposa grabbed the handle before the pitch grew too high. She poured hot water into her cup and let her tea bag immerse. The trailer door creaked as she stepped out into the cool Arizona morning. The sun remained tucked behind red, dusty hills, but the desert was beginning to come to life.

Mariposa sat in her worn chair. She enjoyed this part of the day. Sunlight fought with twilight shadows. Darkness scurried behind rocks and low bushes. Lizards and spiders scampered to find food and shelter, knowing that their veil of safety dwindled by the minute.

The tea cup steamed with fury, so Mariposa placed it on the ground. She picked up her old guitar and placed it in her lap.

"*Buenos días*, old friend," Mariposa said.

Her fingers wrapped around the neck of the guitar, absorbing the frequency of the rough strings. Her right arm rested on the wooden body, a familiar perch for contemplation and patience.

Mariposa's joints stiffened. She wasn't as nimble as she used to be, but decades of repetition were hard to stop. The fingers

11

on her left hand found their frets, forming a C chord. She pushed down, tightening the connection between string and guitar. With her right hand, she strummed.

The strings vibrated, sending a pure note into the empty desert.

"There's nothing quite like the first note," Mariposa's *abuelo* used to say.

She plucked a few strings, breaking up the pure chord into individual parts. Her left hand shifted its configuration into an A minor. She plucked the same pattern of strings.

The combination reminded her of an old Mexican folk song her *abuelo* used to sing. She couldn't remember the exact order of notes and chords and lyrics, but her hands seemed to guide themselves. Slowly, she found the pattern, found the rhythm that sat beneath the notes, felt the vibrations of the strings pulse with her heartbeat. She was connected.

As the sun continued to rise above the rocks, Mariposa forgot about her tea. She forgot about her aching joints. She just played. The same song. Over and over.

The door from a nearby trailer creaked open.

"Mariposa," a young girl said. "That song is beautiful!"

Mariposa shook her focus away from the strings and the mountains and turned her gaze to the girl.

"Thank you, Isabella," Mariposa said.

"Does it have any words?" Isabella asked, walking across the dirt toward Mariposa's trailer.

The guitar rang out a few more notes.

"It does," Mariposa said. "I just don't remember them all."

The girl smiled. She sat on a rock near Mariposa and leaned forward on her elbows.

"Did your parents play the guitar?" Isabella asked.

Mariposa lowered her eyes and shook her head. She began to pluck the strings again.

"Well, the melody is beautiful," Isabella said. "What's it called?"

"*Belleza y Fuerza*," Mariposa said. "My *abuelo* used to play it for me when I was a little girl."

Mariposa continued to strum the chords, interspersing the rhythm with plucked strings and arpeggios. Isabella closed her eyes. She felt the warmth of the sunrise and the mystery of the music. This was one of Isabella's favorite things to do. Sit and listen to Mariposa play her guitar. Isabella's parents were not around much. Mostly, they worked. But sometimes, they didn't work and still stayed away from home for a while. Isabella was used to it. She cooked her own meals. Got herself ready for bed. Woke herself up for school. Walked a mile to the bus stop every morning. And, on the weekends, she sat and listened to Mariposa play the guitar.

Isabella didn't know much about Mariposa, but there was something about the sorrow in her music, the way her fingers labored to pluck each string and form each chord, the way that her sadness vibrated through the guitar and emerged as something beautiful. Isabella felt connected to Mariposa.

An old car rattled down the dirt road, kicking dust into the air. The car pulled up next to Isabella's trailer. A woman emerged. Dark circles hung beneath her eyes, the white parts red with bloodshot webs.

"Isabella," the woman shouted, "I'm going inside to take a nap."

Isabella nodded. Her slight smile masked her disappointment.

Mariposa waited until the trailer door slammed shut. She

stopped strumming her guitar. Clutching the neck of the instrument in her aching palms, Mariposa handed the guitar to Isabella.

"Go ahead," Mariposa said.

Isabella held the guitar, just like she'd seen Mariposa do. Her left hand held the neck. Her right hand draped over the strings.

"Now what?" Isabella asked.

Mariposa smiled.

"I'll teach you," Mariposa said. "First, strum all the strings."

Isabella's hand glided down the metal strings. The pure sound vibrated through the guitar and echoed into the desert and carried on into the horizon.

The Walk

Arkansas

Terrence stepped carefully along the sidewalk. A few puddles had pooled in sloped sections of the concrete. Those were straight up hazards. He watched carefully for cracks, pieces of the sidewalk that had shifted, risen like mountains above tectonic plates. And patches of grass and weeds that had somehow managed to escape to the surface.

All of these were dangerous for his new white shoes.

He had managed to get through the first day of third grade without scuffing them, a feat that he planned to accomplish every day for as long as he could.

His friends had even commented on them before the school day started.

"Nice shoes," Max had said.

"Thanks," Terrence had replied. "I can jump really high in them."

But now his school day was over. He had already parted ways with Max. The other walkers had thinned, branching off to their own streets and neighborhoods. Terrence was alone with his thoughts. His own shoes. His fresh white high tops, lined in black stitching with a black logo, laced to perfection,

15

strapped at the ankle. He might as well have been floating on air and style.

As he turned the corner, he saw the high school looming ahead. He always got excited walking by the high school. It seemed so important, such a symbol of power. Terrence had walked by the high school every day since last year in second grade, when he started walking to and from elementary school. At first, he was intimidated. He was nervous that the high school kids would see him and beat him up.

But they didn't. In fact, they usually didn't notice him, and they were usually in class when he walked by.

Sometimes, a high schooler would comment about how adorable Terrence was. He really hated that. It made him feel like a kid. But he wasn't simply a kid anymore. He was in third grade now, after all. And these fresh white shoes made him feel slightly more grown up.

Terrence's shoes pushed him forward along the sidewalk until he found himself directly in front of the high school. Then, he decided to pause. He wrapped his hands around the iron gate and peered through. His eyes traveled from the lawn up to the imposing staircase, and then climbed to the old brick building.

Terrence's eyes drifted back to his clean shoes, the black contrasted against the white, the fresh leather contrasted against the worn concrete.

His attention was pulled toward the school again. He knew what had happened here. His mother had told him the stories.

Many years ago, schools were segregated by race. This high school was an all-white space. But then, the United States government mandated schools to integrate.

Nine brave Black students walked up to this high school,

ready to begin their school year. But they were greeted by an angry mob of white parents, screaming in their ears, holding signs that aimed to push them away.

Even the governor of Arkansas fought against them. He wanted to keep schools separated by race so badly that he sent the National Guard to keep these nine students from entering the school.

But these students kept trying. Kids battling the government.

President Eisenhower sent the U.S. military in to overrule the governor. Eventually, these nine students got to go into the building.

But it wasn't easy walking through those halls, seeing themselves scrawled across newspapers and on the nightly news, facing scorn and disrespect from white students and parents.

But they did it anyway. They used their courage to overcome fear and make society better.

As Terrence stood there, looking at this building, he couldn't help but wonder how he would have reacted back then. Terrence was a white student; how would he have reacted? He knew how he *hoped* he would have reacted.

How had his mom reacted? What about his grandma?

Terrence remembered a picture he had seen, a picture of a Black student walking to her first day of school. Behind her, a white mother was shouting, her face filled with venom.

Could that have been his own grandmother? Or his grandmother's mother?

He hoped hatred like that couldn't be inherited.

But at the same time, he knew that it was passed down from one generation to the next.

Terrence couldn't understand how so much hatred could

build inside a person, how that hatred could be directed toward a kid who just wanted to learn at school, who just wanted to feel safe and accepted in a school like a kid was supposed to.

He was glad that things had changed.

But had they changed that much?

"Hey, kid," a high schooler said, walking along the fence.

"Hi," Terrence said. Nervousness gripped his voice.

"Cool shoes," the high schooler said.

Terrence looked down at his sneakers. He felt his nervousness begin to subside.

"Thanks," he said.

He thought about the schools in his city. His own school was still mostly white kids. Other schools were mostly Black. The only difference was that, now, this was an unwritten divide. People talked about it like this issue was fixed, like the kids who went to this school solved the issue of racism. But it didn't. Sure, it helped. But, from what Terrence could see, it was still happening. Only now, it simmered under the surface.

Terrence looked at his shoes again. Black against white. New leather against the cracks in the concrete. Old concrete against the newly finished iron bars that enclosed the old school, a school that used to isolate itself, imagining itself superior. Terrence, in his new shoes, a member of a new generation, a new generation that had the power to stop the cycle of hatred, the cycle of injustice. A new generation with a new perspective. A new generation with the vision to atone for the venom they inherited.

The Pier

California

The wooden floorboards were warped, splintered from decades of Southern California sunshine and Pacific Ocean salt water. Rafael took care to lift his feet high as he walked. He didn't want to trip, especially at his age. He walked slowly; his knee joints didn't quite fire like they used to. He carried his fishing pole in one hand, and a tackle box in the other.

Rafael carried his fishing pole with care. It was old. The cork grip had cracks and creases, worn by hundreds of days spent fishing on the pier.

Some men took an overly masculine pride in their ability to catch a fish. Rafael did not. In fact, he rarely hooked a fish. Even when he did, he never told anyone, refusing to use the fish's life to enhance his own mythology. He didn't even tell his wife. She had stopped asking. She understood.

Rafael didn't fish for sport. He didn't keep count of the fish he caught, or the length of the animal.

No. He fished for the quiet.

As he got to his usual spot along the side of the pier, he put his tackle box down and baited his hook, dropping his line down to the ocean. He leaned his pole against the pier's

19

wooden railing. And then he sat on the bench.

The sun began to dip toward the horizon, casting a golden glow along the ocean. Waves crashed. Rafael watched as young surfers rode the waves, harnessing nature's power to propel them forward. Rafael had lived here all his life, but he never learned to surf. Sure, he was drawn to the water, but he never had the desire to move with the force of nature. He preferred to watch it from a distance.

A young couple approached, holding hands as they strolled along the boardwalk. Rafael remembered being young and in love. It was a different kind of love back then, shrouded in mystery. After 40 years of marriage, love transformed. It became an action rather than a state of being. It became a ritual, something to be practiced every day with purpose, not some fleeting sense of joy.

"Excuse me, sir," the young man asked. "Do you know a place around here where my girlfriend and I can grab a drink?"

Rafael smiled, tipping his cap upward to reveal his kind, creased eyes.

"Of course," Rafael said. "There's a bar just at the end of the pier that has a wonderful view of the ocean."

"Thank you," the young man said. "Have a good evening."

Rafael nodded and returned his attention to his fishing pole. His line had drifted close to the pier's support beams, so he reeled it in. After checking his bait, he cast his line out into the ocean again.

Another old man strolled down the pier with fishing gear. His wide-brimmed hat looked new, a stark contrast to Rafael's faded Dodgers cap.

"Hey, Rafe," the old man said. "You catch anything yet?"

Rafael chuckled.

"Not yet, Sergio," Rafael said. "But this sunset is magical."

"Sure is," Sergio said.

Sergio paused to observe the colors of the sky.

"Well, good luck with the fish," Sergio said.

"You too, *hermano*," Rafael said.

Sergio continued his stroll down the boardwalk and eventually set himself up in his usual, solitary spot.

Rafael returned his attention to his fishing pole. He reeled in his line, checked his bait, and cast.

His eyes drifted down the pier toward the shore. Tall palm trees swayed along the street. Families played on the beach, way in the distance.

Rafael still couldn't believe that his wife had been gone for over a year. It felt like yesterday that he held her hand for the last time before the cancer overtook her.

But 40 years was a long time. All 40 years were good. Most had been great.

Rafael reeled in his line, checked the bait, and cast again. He watched the surfers ride waves; they looked so free.

As the sun dipped below the ocean, Rafael reeled in his line and packed his tackle box. He walked slowly back down the pier. The same pier that he and his wife used to walk along every Sunday after church, holding hands, sometimes laughing, sometimes quiet, always practicing love.

The Snowboarder

Colorado

Marley's feet dangled over the cold metal chair lift. Her snowboard was strapped to one foot, its weight pulling her down toward the mountain far below. She sat alone on the lift. She had navigated her way from the center of the mountain where most of the people spent most of their day. Instead, she had found an isolated set of runs around the side, a lift that few people bothered to seek.

The wind was calm, but the motion of the lift caused a light breeze, chilling Marley's neck and nose, the only exposed pieces of her skin. Her goggled, tinted orange, gave the already sunny sky a tropical hue, like a vintage photograph.

The lift ride was long, giving Marley time to look without feeling rushed. She heard nothing. No music pumped from the ski bar. No shouting from excited kids or obnoxious old guys trying to relive their glory days on the mountain.

Nothing.

Just her and her own thoughts. A perfect time to consider her next move.

Marley only had a few months left of high school. As her senior year dwindled, she found herself left with options. And,

22

within these options, she found herself suspended in a state of decision paralysis. She needed a day on the mountain to clear her mind.

The city had the ability to constantly consume her thoughts. Her phone, her friends, her homework, her shows, her apps. All of these distractions, these pressures that blocked her from actually thinking a thought.

She needed the mountain.

Some snowboarders carved silently below her, painting graceful arches in the untouched snow canvas.

The chair lift climbed higher.

Marley had been accepted to a college near home. It was a safe bet. Cheaper. But she had also been accepted to a school across the country, to a state she'd never seen. Which wasn't saying much. Marley had hardly left Colorado. She knew that the country and the world had so much more to offer, so much more to explore, but the choice to make a move, to set off on an unknown path, seemed unwise.

Or, maybe just uncomfortable.

Money wasn't the issue. Her family could pay for lift tickets, snowboards, and a car. Tuition was no obstacle. Plus, she'd gotten some partial academic scholarships.

The decision itself was the tough part. The fork in the road.

Marley heard the familiar rattle of the churning chair lift gears. She watched as the chair neared the end of the line, anticipating the approach. Sitting forward in her seat, Marley placed her free foot on the board. As she hovered above the snow, she dropped off the chair and slid comfortably to the top of the run. She sat in the snow and strapped her free foot into her binding.

From the top of the mountain, she looked out over the trees.

Her eyes followed the mountain down to the road below, a thin line carved through the valley.

She vaulted herself up on her board and balanced perpendicularly to the run. The wind whipped, unobstructed by trees on the mountain's bald peak. Marley allowed herself to sway with the wind, lost in the quiet. She looked around. No one else was here. Just her.

Perfect, she thought.

Marley jumped, and her board raised off the snow. Her board landed and faced the run. Momentum carried Marley forward. She controlled the momentum, carving on her heels, and then her toes.

As she increased her speed, she focused her attention ahead of her where, soon, the run would split in two. Marley knew she would have to make a decision.

The run on the right was familiar. She knew it well. She had taken this run many times before, almost out of habit. Marley enjoyed the run, its consistent slope, its openness, its incline on the edge. She could go fast, but she could control it.

The run on the left was less familiar. She wasn't sure if she had ever taken it before. It looked like it might weave through some trees. But it looked untouched, which left the potential for fresh powder.

Digging her heels into the snow, she carved left.

The run dropped her into a steep, smooth slope. It funneled her into a narrow chute before she released into a wide, untouched run. She floated on fresh powder, casting a wake of frozen waves behind her. Evergreens rose high above her. She couldn't see the lift; she couldn't hear other runs.

Marley felt free.

The Politics

Connecticut

Nia turned off the television. She couldn't handle the national news anymore. Too much negative messaging. Too many dramatic opinions instead of actual reporting. One station criticized a politician while the other station blindly praised the same action. Split down party lines. Die hard party fans.

Every. Single. Day.

Nia was done.

But, at the same time, she was just getting started.

This polarization had prompted her to run for office. Nothing wild like a United States Senator or anything. Nothing national. At least not yet.

Nia was running for city council.

She majored in political science in college, but she got a job at a nursing home right after graduation and never left. That was five years ago. She enjoyed it, but the experience had also shown her the pitfalls of the industry. And of a society that chose not to care for its elders, choosing to export them instead.

This certainly hadn't trained her for a career in politics or public policy-making. She recognized her own inexperience, but she hoped that her enthusiasm would make up for it.

And she was running against an incumbent, someone who was a name in the community. One of those names that came with political history behind it.

Nia's phone rang, starling her from a dive into self-pity.

"Hey, Mom," Nia said.

"Have any results rolled in yet?" she asked.

"Nothing new yet," Nia said. "As of this morning, I was down a little, but there weren't enough votes counted to reveal anything meaningful."

Nia stood and began to pace around her small apartment. She stopped at the window and watched traffic speed by.

"We should know something more concrete soon, though," Nia continued. "Mark is going to call me when he has some actual numbers."

Nia lifted her thumb nail to her teeth and began to nibble.

"Well, honey," her mom said, "whatever happens, know that I'm proud of you."

Nia felt tears well up in her eyes. The cars outside became blurry.

"Don't expect too much," Nia said. "I know I probably don't have a shot at winning this thing."

"But you'll do a damn good job if you do," her mom said.

Nia hung up the phone and stared out the window. Sun rays from the fading light beamed into her dusty apartment. She held her tears back. She couldn't cry today.

She wanted to check her computer, or the local news station. She wanted to see how her numbers were looking now that votes were being tallied with full force. But she held herself back. Looking at the ever-shifting numbers would just enhance her anxiety.

She checked her phone.

6:04 p.m.

The evening news was starting. The votes would be showing reliable numbers at this point.

Her phone vibrated, so she looked again. A text from her assistant.

"It's close," Mark wrote.

Nia felt her pulse quicken. In some way, she hoped for a blowout, that way, she wouldn't allow herself to get her hopes up. It would almost be worse to lose by a few votes than to get swept. Either way, she knew she would lose.

But she hoped she would win. Nia had big plans for her time on city council. And her plans were simple, easy to initiate, and effective for everyone. Things like a balanced budget, more transparency, more compromise, and a focus on society's most vulnerable people. She wanted to pass laws, not because it would benefit her career, but because they were the right things to do.

Her opponent had been entrenched in city politics for decades. He was loyal to certain groups, certain lobbies, certain positions. Nia had met him a few times. He was nice enough in person, charming with a dashing smile, but he would say anything to get a vote.

As Nia stared out the window, the sun dipped behind the buildings. She moved back over to her couch and dove into a pillow. She turned on the television and found a movie channel. It was playing an old film, black and white. She let the old noise lull her to sleep.

Her phone buzzed, snapping her from a dream. Her apartment was dark. The sun had set completely. With blurry eyes, she looked at her phone.

Mark, she thought. *I hope he can break the news to me gently.*

"Nia!" Mark shouted through the earpiece. "Are you seeing this?"

Nia looked at her television. Another black-and-white film had started since she dozed off. Someone was giving an impassioned speech to a courtroom.

"Seeing what?" Nia asked, still half-dazed.

"The results," Mark said. "They're not fully counted yet, but..."

Nia snapped from her hypnosis and grabbed the remote. She flipped the channel to the local news. And then she saw it.

"It looks like I'm winning," she said in disbelief.

"You sure are," Mark said. "Unless almost every other vote goes against you, it's safe to say that you've won. The newspaper just called me and said that they're going to declare you the winner."

As he finished his sentence, the television shifted. Nia's face appeared on the screen. Her name appeared beneath her image. And beneath that: winner.

"Mark," Nia said. "We won!"

"*You* won, Nia," Mark said. "They voted for you, and you won!"

Nia walked to the window and looked out above the dark city. Traffic lights flashed from red to green. Street lights covered the concrete in an orange hue. Headlights from cars sped around concrete buildings lit by internal office lights. People, moving throughout their days, trying to make the world better than it was before they woke up, reflecting on the way they could impact the world tomorrow.

"Now what do I do?" Nia asked.

"The best you can," Mark said.

The Return

Delaware

The plane jolted as it touched down on the runway. Jacob shifted in his seat. Spacious, even by first class standards. He finished his drink and slid his laptop into his briefcase, along with his notebook and charts.

He moved through the crowded airport terminal, weaving between people who lazily strolled to their gates. He didn't have time for that. He had places to be.

Jacob arrived at baggage claim and found his suitcase almost immediately. He yanked it off the conveyor belt and rolled it outside. He scanned the crowd for a man in a black suit holding a card with his name on it. Private car. The only way to roll.

As he searched the sidewalk for his chauffeur, his eyes narrowed.

"Dad?" Jacob said.

His father ran toward Jacob and embraced him.

"Why are you here?" Jacob asked. "I told you that I ordered a chauffeur."

His dad smiled, a smile that suggested compassion and frustration simultaneously.

"I called and canceled," his dad said. "I wanted to pick you up myself. You don't come home that often. I had to pick you myself."

Jacob smiled, a veneer to shield what he was really thinking. He grabbed his suitcase and placed it in the trunk, and then slid into the passenger seat. His father climbed behind the wheel, clicked his seat belt, and slowly pressed the gas pedal.

"How are things in New York?" his dad asked.

Jacob looked toward his father. Somehow, Jacob defaulted to angst, even as a 30-year-old.

"Fine," Jacob said.

The car moved away from the airport. Jacob allowed his attention to drift out the window. He watched as airplanes departed from the runway, one right after the other.

"Are you excited to be back home?" his dad asked. "It's been a while. I'll bet there are some people you want to see. Places you want to visit."

"Honestly, I'm pretty tired from the flight," Jacob said. "I'd rather get some sleep, get the wedding over with, and go back to New York."

His dad nodded his head and gripped the steering wheel.

Jacob hadn't returned to his small hometown in years for a reason. He wanted to leave the past behind him. As a kid, Jacob's dream had always been to leave. There was nothing in this town. He always knew that he needed to go to the big city if he wanted to make anything of himself. His hometown, as far as Jacob was concerned, was dead, like going back in time.

Sure, the town had a movie theater, but it only played second-chance films, and the ticket prices were far too cheap to suggest any real value. His childhood town had a grocery store, but it looked run down. A decent high school sports program;

the community supported it, but they never got any attention outside of the town. No notable city ball caps or t-shirts to represent pride. As if there was any pride to take.

Jacob took no pride in his small town. He went to great lengths to hide his origins whenever big city people asked where he was from. "Delaware," he'd say, and leave it at that.

He left after high school, went to a major college, something to give his origin story some notoriety. Graduate school after that. And then, a big job at a famous financial firm in New York.

And he tried as hard as he could to stay away from home. He had returned a handful of times. Once for a wedding. Once for a funeral. Once for Christmas. He was always too busy to make it back to Delaware for something as minor as a birthday.

But his younger sister was getting married. Not something he could turn down. Of course, she was getting married in their family's childhood church. The reception would be at their childhood community center.

And, of course, he would be forced to interact with the same small town people he had tried so hard to get away from.

"Well, here we are," his dad said.

The car pulled into the driveway of Jacob's childhood home, a small one-level house with a decent front yard.

Before he opened the door, Jacob's father nodded toward a neighboring house.

"There's Mr. Ellis," he said. "You remember him, don't you?"

"Of course I do," Jacob said.

He looked at the old man standing in the yard. His ancient clippers pruned a small bush. His joints and muscles strained to clip a thin branch.

"But let's move into the house quickly," Jacob said. "I'm not in the mood for neighborhood small talk. I don't see the value in it."

Jacob's father scowled, holding his gaze on Jacob for a beat longer than Jacob felt comfortable with. Jacob opened the car door to break the stare. His father opened his side of the car and moved to the trunk to grab Jacob's suitcase. Jacob feigned a slow pace, allowing his father to carry his heavy bag.

As his father moved along the driveway, Mr. Ellis stepped away from his plant and walked into Jacob's yard.

"Well, if it isn't the Prodigal Son," Mr. Ellis said. "Returned for his little sister's big day."

Jacob wanted to increase his walking speed and pretend that he didn't hear Mr. Ellis. In fact, if Mr. Ellis had been a few feet back, he might have. But Mr. Ellis was closing in on the driveway with surprising velocity for someone so frail. Jacob had no choice.

"Yeah," Jacob said. "Back for my sister's wedding."

Mr. Ellis scouted Jacob, searching his face for his true intentions.

"Does it feel good to be home for a while?" Mr. Ellis asked.

"Not really," Jacob said. "There's not much going on here compared to what I'm used to these days."

Mr. Ellis smiled and leaned against the car.

"And that's what makes this place so beautiful," Mr. Ellis said.

He held his smile, a smile that took him back decades, a smile that held memories and emotions and happiness within it.

Jacob raised an eyebrow. He dug into his vocabulary banks to find a snappy comeback, but words evaded his search. In its place, Mr. Ellis's remark sunk into his thoughts, rolled around in his mind.

Maybe this place, this slow, gentle, humble place, was beautiful.

"Jacob!" his sister shouted from the doorstep. "I'm so glad you made it!"

Maybe this place was precisely the reminder Jacob needed.

The Sports Car

Florida

The sun pierced through the humidity, baking and steaming the concrete that ran along the beach. Palm trees sunk beneath the midday heat, weighed down by dense air.

Warner watched the red light. He silently begged it to turn green. He wanted to beat the guy next to him. Not like he was in a race. But he wanted to speed along the street that lined the beach, the street with the coolest, youngest people. He wanted to accelerate in his sports car, everyone's attention on his engine, on his power.

He knew the light would change soon. He revved his engine and looked at the guy next to him in an old four-door mid-level car.

"I got this," Warner said to himself.

The light turned green. Warner slammed his foot against the pedal and smoked the car next to him. The engine roared. Wind flooded through the interior. Pride swelled in Warner's chest.

And then he hit the brakes for the impending red light.

The four-door car pulled up next to Warner slowly.

"I bet you feel pretty cool," the guy shouted out the window.

Warner kept his eyes forward, feeling slightly embarrassed. He looked the other way toward the beach. He thought he noticed a woman looking at his car. Another swell of pride flooded his mind.

And he needed that pride wherever he could get it.

Last week, he turned 42.

"Happy birthday, sweetie," his mother had said, her voice crackling through the phone speaker.

"Thanks, Mom," Warner said, unsuccessfully suppressing the sadness in his voice.

That was before he had his new sports car.

As soon as he had hung up the phone, he went to the dealership and bought the red status symbol. He already had a boat. He bought that a year ago. He had used it a few times, sticking mostly to the shore off the Florida coast, hoping that people would notice and want to come aboard.

They didn't.

Somehow, he thought that this new car would get him the fulfillment he craved. And looking ahead at 42 made him realize that he had so much he had wanted to accomplish, but hadn't. Somehow, in his mind, he had worked himself up to believe that everything needed to be accomplished by 40. Somehow, he saw the rest of life disintegrating.

So he bought a boat.

And then he bought some nice shoes. And then some tailored suits. He never wore the suits. His job required casual clothes. But the suits made him feel important.

At least temporarily.

So he bought some more shoes.

When that didn't give him the fulfillment he wanted, when he saw 42 approaching, he set his eyes on the car.

Maybe that would replace the void left by his ex-wife.

"I thought we'd be living in a mansion on the ocean by now," she used to say.

"Soon," Warner would say. "My big break is coming."

But his big break never happened. He remained at his mid-level job at a mid-level company in a mid-sized office managing underwhelming accounts. He made enough money to support his wife. They owned a small home and a functional car. But that wasn't the goal.

To compete in Florida's high-level society, Warner knew that he needed certain symbols to show his value. He needed the clothes and the shoes. He needed the house. Eventually, houses. Plural. He needed the boat. And, most importantly, he needed the car.

When these things never came, his wife moved on.

So, there he sat at the stoplight in his red sports car, unfulfilled and deeply in debt. His windows were rolled down. The ocean breeze floated through the car interior, blowing his thinning hair. His stereo thumped, bass reverberating, hoping to attract attention from beachgoers. An angry driver sat in the car next to him, still fuming about losing the unofficial race from the previous stoplight.

The light turned green. The angry driver sped forward, and then sped through the next green light, and then turned, out of sight. But Warner moved slowly. He saw an empty parking spot up against the beach's boardwalk, so he pulled in. His unfamiliarity with a manual transmission jerked his car a little. He removed his expensive suit jacket and his tie. He had no need to wear them anyway. He removed his watch and shoved it in the glove compartment.

He got out of the car and stepped onto the boardwalk. With

no plan in mind, he simply walked, allowing the sun to warm his face and the sea breeze to cool it.

Eventually, he noticed a small bar that edged against the beach. He strolled in and found an empty seat at the bar along the sand. After ordering a beer, Warner placed his car keys on the bar top. The car's iconic logo faced up.

An old man sat next to him. His face was tanned and deeply wrinkled beneath a white beard. His cap tipped upward, revealing his bronzed forehead. He lowered his sunglasses and looked at the logo on the car keys.

"I used to have one of those," the old man said.

Warner turned and nodded.

"It's a nice ride," Warner said.

The old man smirked and lifted his sunglasses again.

"It sure was," the old man said.

"What happened to your car?" Warner asked. "Upgraded to a newer model?"

The old man smirked again.

"I realized I didn't need it," the old man said. "Unfortunately, I realized that too late."

Warner raised an eyebrow.

"How so?" Warner asked.

The old man's smirk dropped into a frown.

"Why do you think I'm sitting here all by myself?"

The Phone

Georgia

Levi sat in the metal chair outside the restaurant. He resisted the urge to look at his phone, the urge to forge a connection with the outside world. Instead, he opened the menu. His friend would arrive soon, but he wanted to have an idea of his order before his friend arrived. He liked to feel prepared.

The club sandwich stuck out. That was it. A club sandwich with a side of potato chips and a Coke.

Barry hadn't arrived yet, so Levi gave in an pulled out his phone. Not because he needed to, but because he wanted to. There was nothing else to do, anyway. He scrolled through one of his social media feeds. A few posts of family photos from old high school acquaintances that he never talked to anymore.

But that wasn't what drove Levi to scroll. No, not connection to old friends. He was here for the news.

He scrolled down and saw a headline that made his anger flare. The headline read: Federal Government Uses Clean Energy Vehicles to Spy on Citizens.

I knew it, he thought. *The government has been running surveillance on us the whole time. Climate change was a hoax.*

Levi clicked the article link. He read the first few sentences, which confirmed the headline's claim. The article hadn't cited a reliable source yet, but the website wouldn't have printed it if it wasn't true. Besides, the government wouldn't make sources available for something this nefarious.

He jumped back to his social media feed and scrolled again.

Another headline grabbed his attention: Government Using Nanorobot Vaccines to Track Civilians.

Of course they are, he thought.

Levi clicked on the link. He read the first two sentences and looked at the picture. The story was sensational, almost too absurd to believe. But it had to be true. The name of a major city featured prominently in the title of the publication. He'd never heard of it before, but it was probably one of those news sites that worked underground to expose the truth that the mainstream media tried to hide.

He moved back to his social media feed.

"Hey, Levi!" Barry said as he walked toward the table.

Levi lifted his gaze from his phone screen. He placed his phone on the table face up so he could still see his screen, just in case a crucial notification appeared. Barry sat down across from Levi. He thought about removing his sunglasses, but the sunshine was too bright, so he left them on.

"What's up, man?" Barry said.

"Same stuff," Levi said.

Barry smiled and waited for Levi to reveal more detail, or perhaps ask how he was doing. But nothing came. So, Barry grabbed the menu and began to sift through the options.

"It's been a while since we got together," Barry said. "Seems like you've been busy with work."

"A little busy, I guess," Levi said.

Barry had tried to get together with Levi every month for the past two years, but Levi usually had an excuse. Mostly work-related, but sometimes not.

They had been best friends in high school. Levi was an outgoing leader on the basketball team, book smart, friendly with lots of groups within the high school hierarchy. They went their separate ways for college. Barry traveled to the West Coast, while Levi remained in Georgia. They stayed in contact. When Barry moved back home to Georgia, he immediately met up with Levi.

But something had shifted. The look in Levi's eyes had become cynical. Levi was extremely active in his online life, portraying himself as a staunch idealist, reposting and liking and sending. While his online persona was active, his actual life was far from it.

"What have you been up to besides work?" Barry asked.

"I read a lot these days," Levi said.

"Awesome," Barry said. What books have you gotten into?"

"I mostly just read articles," Levi said.

Barry nodded. He had seen some of the articles that Levi posted on social media. A few years ago, they started out as defined stances on issues, but they had gradually grown more extreme, more unreliable.

"What do you read?" Barry asked.

"All kinds of things," Levi said. "There are so many online publications out there that are actually exposing the truth. None of this biased, water-down mainstream media stuff. I'm talking underground."

Barry felt his temperature begin to rise. Luckily, a waiter appeared to take their order. Levi was prepared: club sandwich, potato chips, and Coke. Barry looked at a few options before deciding: hamburger, fries, and sweet tea.

"I'll be back soon with your lunches," the waiter said.

Barry thanked the waiter. Levi's attention had drifted toward his phone again. Barry noticed, feeling slightly irritated.

"What are some things you've read recently?" Barry asked, trying to find some common ground.

Levi smirked and looked at the cars passing by.

"The government is spying on us, man," Levi said. "That's what the vaccines are for. The government is forcing everyone to get these vaccines, and they're putting nanorobots in them. That way, they can track our every move."

Barry threw his head back and laughed. But his laughter subsided after he realized that Levi was serious.

"The government is *not* using vaccines to track our movement," Barry said.

"You don't think the government spies on us?" Levi asked. "That must be your West Coast education talking."

Barry smiled and shook his head.

"They already track us," Barry said. "And they didn't need to force us to take vaccines to do it.

Barry tapped Levi's phone screen.

"In fact, you volunteered to pay one thousand dollars to carry around a tracking device," Barry said. "And trolls from who-knows-where are brainwashing you through that same tracking device."

Levi picked his phone up, handling it as if it were a delicate crystal.

"There's more to life than that little screen, man," Barry said. "Get your mind off your phone and social media so much. Start living again."

The waiter appeared with a tray of food and drinks. He

placed the hamburger and sweet tea in front of Barry. Then, he put the club sandwich and Coke in front of Levi. When Barry looked at the table, he noticed that Levi had put the phone away in his pocket. And he thought he saw a hint of life return to Levi's eyes.

The Tree

Hawaii

The old man's feet dug into the sand as he moved from the grass to the beach. The sun was rising to the East, casting orange hues across the clear sky. The ocean nearly reflected the sunrise, but its wild waves churned the water, giving it a deep blue color. The wind blew gently, a calm sea breeze that sent the smell of salt through the humid air.

He sat down against a palm tree, the same palm tree that he leaned against nearly every morning for the last ten years. The tree trunk had a slight curve that allowed his back to sink into a perfect, comfortable posture.

Surfers prepared their boards on the beach. Some surfers were already in the water catching early morning waves. Not huge waves, but big enough.

"Hey, old man," a young surfer said. "Should have a nice set coming in today."

"I hope so," the old man said. "Enjoy your time out there."

The young surfer smiled.

"Hopefully we'll give you something fun to watch," the young surfer said.

The young surfer joined a small group of early morning

surfers on the beach. He put his board down, tossed his small backpack in the sand, and talked with his friends before running out into the waves.

The old man used to be one of them: an early morning surfer.

Before the old man found his palm tree, he came to this beach nearly every morning to surf for an hour before work. The same routine for decades.

As his joints became creaky and his body began to wrinkle and his stamina began to fade, the old man decided that it was time to put his surfboard away. The wrinkles around his eyes grew deeper, the curved posture in his back more pronounced. He found himself walking slow and methodical, not the vibrant bounce he was used to.

But he couldn't give up the atmosphere of surfing. There was something about the beach, the waves, the ocean, the frequency that emanated from the surfboard that drew him back to the beach. And it was that something that pulled him to the palm tree each morning to watch surfers.

As he sat against his tree, he filled himself with simultaneous peace and envy. Watching the surfers go through their routine, through their methodical approach to waves, filled him with a connection between humanity and nature, between surfer and ocean, but he wished that he could get back out there and surf like he used to.

And, oh, how he used to surf.

His hair was long back then, down to his shoulder blades. In high school, he used to come to this beach just before sunrise. Sometimes there were other surfers, but usually he was alone. He would spend a few minutes sitting in the sand, simply watching the ocean to see how the waves were moving that day. Then, he would paddle out beyond the break. He enjoyed sitting on his board, watching the sun rise over the open ocean, thinking about everything and nothing at the same time.

And then he would sense the perfect wave. He looked for certain things, particular features in the tide that gave it away, but mostly it was a feeling.

He would paddle hard toward the beach, allowing the wave to pick him up. Then, he would pop onto his feet, effortless. He loved the feeling of the board dropping into the wave, working *with* the wave's force instead of against it.

And then he would just ride.

He felt connected to the ocean, connected to the land that had raised him, and connected to the culture and the people that had come before him. When the Hawaiian language was banned in schools, so many pieces of Hawaiian cultural expression began to fade. But surfing remained as a connection that spanned generations.

And there wasn't one right way to surf. Everyone had their own style, their own way to express themselves, finding their own path within their cultural expression.

And he loved it. With every wave, he felt it.

So he kept the same routine. An hour or two every morning before school. His exercise, his meditation, his form of independence, his form of protest, his connection to who he was.

When he was done in the ocean, he walked on the beach back to his car.

"Nice ride," a classmate would say.

"Thanks," he would say.

Sometimes, they exchanged words in Hawaiian, sometimes in English. Sometimes, they exchanged ideas without using words at all.

After high school, he got a job bussing tables at a beachside restaurant. One of those restaurants that didn't take itself too seriously. It only had a few items on the menu, but they had been perfected over decades of fine-tuning. Luckily, the restaurant opened around ten in the morning, so he could keep the same surfing routine going.

As he got older, he moved from bussing tables to waiting tables. And continued to do that until he was an old man.

"Don't drop those plates, old man," a customer said.

"I haven't dropped one yet," he said.

But he was worried. His strength was beginning to fade. His joints were beginning to feel stiff.

When the plates of food started to shake, he knew that it was time to move on. And around that same time, he realized that he could no longer surf.

But he couldn't give up surfing, not completely.

So, every morning, he kept his routine. He went to the beach at dawn. Instead of bringing his own surfboard, he just sat against his palm tree and watched as younger generations expressed themselves through surfing.

Today, that young surfer was working waves, one right after the next. His balance between exerting his own force and using the wave's momentum was masterful. As that young surfer came in from the water, he tucked his board beneath his arm and walked up the beach.

"How'd I look out there?" the young surfer asked.

The old man smiled.

"You looked like you were at peace."

The Goal

Laila dribbled the ball down the field. She faked left. The defender stayed with her. Laila dashed to the right. Her defender stayed with her. But the defender had overcompensated, throwing her momentum too far across her body.

Got her, Laila thought.

Laila threw her shoulder to the right, forcing the defender to fully commit. And then, Laila dribbled left. Her defender spun, tripping over her own feet. Laila took one long dribble and sprinted forward toward the goal.

The keeper danced on her toes. Laila saw the nervousness in her eyes.

As Laila moved inside the box, she set the ball up. Placing her left foot next to the ball, her right leg propelled forward. She'd practiced this shot thousands of times. The motion was automatic. Smooth. Effortless.

Laila watched the ball. It moved in slow motion, rising above the grass, bending toward the corner of the goal. The keeper dove. The ball floated over the keeper's gloves.

It's in, Laila thought.

But the ball kept sailing. Over the keeper's hands, and then over the bar, and then out of bounds.

Laila's eyes widened.

"I missed," she whispered.

The whistle blew three times. The game was over.

We tied, Laila thought.

She walked over to the sideline. Her head hung low.

"It's alright," Coach said. "We didn't lose."

Laila raised an eyebrow.

We tied, Laila thought. *That's even worse*.

Luckily, it was only the first game of the middle school soccer tournament. As an eighth grader, this would be Laila's last contest before she moved on to high school. And that's when things would get even more serious. The way she played in high school would dictate which college she could go to. And the way she played in college would determine her likelihood of going pro.

And it all stemmed from how she played in middle school.

Laila's parents had an awning set up in the parking lot near their car. They were sitting in lawn chairs, drinking soda.

As Laila approached, her dad stood and offered up his seat. He smiled at her. Laila forced a smile back.

"Good game, honey," Laila's mom said.

Laila dropped her head as she sat in the seat.

"I missed the shot," Laila said. "And, because of that, we tied."

Laila's parents looked at each other with unspoken communication. Her dad knelt down next to her and put his hand on her knee.

"Sweetie," her dad said, "I understand how frustrating that is. Trust me. I've been there."

"But you have another game," her mom said. "You'll have another shot. And this time, you just might make it."

Laila looked up at her parents. She felt a smile rise to her face, but her stubbornness forced that smile to remain unseen.

She reached into the small cooler that her parents brought and grabbed a peanut butter and jelly sandwich and a water bottle. She ate in silence. When her sandwich was done, she stood and stepped out of the shade.

"Time to go warm up for our next game," Laila said. "We're on Field Three."

Both of her parents smiled.

"Good luck, sweetie," her dad said.

"Have fun," her mom said.

Laila stomped through the grass. Her mom's words echoed in her mind.

Have fun, Laila thought. *How can I have fun when I miss a shot, a shot that might take me to college on a scholarship one day?*

Her head began to ache from squinting, partly from the bright sunlight, but partially from her forced scowl. As she approached Field Three, her coach and a few teammates had already arrived.

"Laila!" Coach shouted. "Did you get something to eat?"

Laila nodded.

"Good," Coach said.

Laila's usual confidence and joy had been replaced by discouragement. And Coach noticed.

"Come here, Laila," Coach said.

Laila raised an eyebrow, but she jogged over to her coach.

"I know you're upset about missing that shot," Coach said.

Laila nodded. She didn't want to talk about that shot.

"It happens all the time," Coach continued. "Even the best players in the world miss those shots. What separates the good players from the great players is how they respond. Good players let a bad shot get inside their head. They start thinking too much and take things too seriously. The *great* players remember their bad shots and use that memory as fuel for the next time they have an opportunity. They grow from their mistakes."

Laila looked up at her coach.

"And you know something else?" Coach said. "You're only in eighth grade. You're going to make a lot of mistakes. And you have plenty of time to worry about the future later. For now, get out there and enjoy this beautiful game."

A smile finally escaped onto Laila's face.

"So, Laila," Coach said. "Are you going to be great today?"

Laila nodded. Coach patted her on the shoulder. The momentum sent Laila onto the field. A teammate passed her the ball. Laila passed it back. The pass felt lighter, and so did the weight on her mind.

After a few minutes of kicking the ball around, Laila jogged and stretched. And then, she lined up at midfield. The next game was about to start.

The whistle blew. Laila dashed forward. Her midfielder was dribbling down the opposite side of the field. Laila feigned left, drawing her defender toward the middle of the field, and then Laila cut back to the right, slipping behind her defender with full speed. Laila's midfielder saw Laila start her run. She sent the ball flying over the defensive back line.

Laila sprinted, passing the last defender. The ball landed at the top of the box. The opposing keeper came off the line to grab the ball, but Laila was already there. She tapped the ball out of the keeper's reach. She gathered the ball with her right foot, and then she let it fly.

Goal, Laila thought.

As Laila jogged back to midfield, her teammates ran toward her to celebrate. For once, Laila couldn't see ahead of this moment. And she didn't want to. The feeling of being on this field with these girls made her feel light. Nothing mattered. Not making the high school team, not getting a college scholarship, not making it to the pros. For once, she absorbed the present. The only thing that mattered was enjoying the game.

The Suburbs

Illinois

The smell of freshly mowed grass wafted through the kitchen's open window, and the golden hue of morning reflected off of the copper tea pot on the stove. Erin stared out the window. Her husband had just pulled out of the driveway. His gray SUV rolled along the pavement until it disappeared into the tree-lined street. He was on his way to work. Just another Tuesday.

The house was already clean. The house cleaner came on Monday, and the kids hadn't created too much of a hurricane to warrant another thorough cleaning. Erin had plans to grab coffee with another mom from Rachel's second grade class, but that wasn't until later.

Just another Tuesday.

Erin felt a wave of confinement overcome her mind, a sense that she was somehow trapped in this cell of a house, this facade of a street.

This feeling wasn't new. It happened every weekday when her husband left for work, when her kids left for school. It even hung around when her family returned home, sulking in the back of her mind.

And she wasn't sure why. Of course, she had thought about this feeling often. She had talked about it occasionally with other moms over coffee, but those conversations usually lended themselves better to superficial subjects.

"What am I going to do today?" Erin asked.

She watched an old man walk his dog along the sidewalk. He had headphones on, drowning out the world's noises. He seemed to float, carefree.

Erin broke from her window gaze and looked in the refrigerator. She grabbed a small yogurt and poured some berries and granola in it.

"Another nutritious breakfast," Erin said.

As she ate, she scrolled through her phone, finally opening up her calendar.

"Mostly blank again," Erin said.

She finished her yogurt and put the bowl in the sink. Grabbing her coffee mug, she wandered back to the window. Her mug was empty, but she held it close for comfort.

As she looked out the window again, she wondered what it would be like to live in the city instead of the suburbs.

She imagined the steady stream of cars, stopping and starting at traffic lights and stop signs on every block, a low hum of rhythm and melody echoing off the concrete high rises and iron fire escapes. She imagined the palette of people that she would interact with as she walked to corner coffee shops. She imagined the art and the vibrancy and the smell of rain on warm concrete in the summer.

And then she looked out her window.

Perfectly manicured grass. Newly paved streets, just wide enough for two midsize SUVs to pass each other without acknowledging the other's existence. Trees lined the street, each tree pruned and precisely distanced from the tree before it.

No flaws. No character. No nuance.

"What makes my street any different from the thousands of American suburbs?" Erin asked.

She looked around her kitchen, afraid that an answer would come echoing toward her.

No answer came. Instead, she answered the question herself.

"Nothing," she said.

Nothing defined her street as being different from any other suburb in the country. Nothing stood out that made this street *this* street as opposed to *that* street.

Within the city limits of Chicago, neighborhoods and streets had character, their own flavor. Lawns weren't perfectly manicured. Many houses didn't even have lawns. Many houses weren't even *houses*, just stacks of apartments and condos. Weeds grew from cracks in the concrete. Graffiti adorned the brick walls of buildings and restaurants, whether the owners wanted that artwork there or not. The train reverberated above homes and offices and sidewalks. Cars honked at each other between stop lights. And skyscrapers towered above the city, blocking the sun from entering, from casting its light on the day.

But there was something about the imperfections of the city that made it so alluring. Nothing was ever the same from block to block, from building to building. Nothing was perfectly manicured or eerily symmetrical. And that made it exciting.

Erin looked out her window into the sterile environment of her suburban street. The feeling of confinement began to enclose her mind again. Her vision tunneled. She stumbled back from the window and leaned against the kitchen island.

Reaching for a glass, she filled it with water from the sink and drank.

And then, her vision returned through the window to the tree-lined street outside.

"Enough," Erin said.

She put on her shoes, grabbed a light jacket, and snatched her car keys. She walked outside. Standing by her car door, she inhaled.

Just go, Erin thought. *Just for a few hours.*

With no plan, Erin opened her car door and started the engine. She backed out of the driveway and drove away from her house, watching it disappear in the rearview mirror. And her feeling of confinement dissipated along with it.

An old soul song hummed on the radio. She turned up the volume and rolled her window down, speeding along toward the center of Chicago.

* * *

The sun began to set, casting long shadows across the tree-lined street. Erin reflected on her time in the city, her getaway from the mundanity of her daily routine.

Her cappuccino at the corner coffee shop. The barista crafted a small heart in the foam. She sat outside the coffee shop and watched people walk by, people of all different shades and sizes.

Her stroll through the park. She stepped over uneven concrete, looking at the trees and absorbing the motion of the small waves that came in from somewhere out in the lake.

Her time was spent staring into the warped mirror statue. She saw herself reflected in ways that her own bathroom mirror could never accomplish.

Her friendly wave to a man who might have lived on the park bench. Despite his circumstances, he still went out of his way to be friendly.

Her discussion with an old woman who knitted on a stoop. Erin leaned against the wire fence, listening to the old woman's stories about the neighborhood. And how the neighborhood was changing. First, white people left for the suburbs. Home values plummeted. Now, they were coming back with money, buying homes for cheap and pushing Black people out. Erin had never considered this before.

As Erin pulled into her own driveway, she saw her husband's car. For once, she wasn't home to greet him at the door. For once, he would be forced to take ownership over his own loneliness in the house. And picking up the kids. And maybe over dinner.

She opened the front door. Her husband turned to her, his eyes tired from an hour of kids and dinner and routine and isolation and domestic responsibility.

Erin smirked.

"How was your day?" she asked.

The Road

Indiana

The road stretched outward, expanding infinitely in front of the windshield. The truck engine hummed, straining under the weight of the cargo it towed behind it. The sun hung high in the air. Open road. No shadows. Just the way Ben preferred to drive through Indiana.

"It's another warm autumn afternoon here in northern Indiana," the radio hummed. *"It looks like traffic is light from Fort Wayne all the way into Indianapolis."*

"Good," Ben said. "I can't get stuck in rush hour traffic moving south. I can't be late."

Ben wasn't from Indiana, but he spent enough time driving his truck from one end to the other and back again on his way to or from somewhere else. The state had become like a second home. He knew the roads better than his map did. He knew which gas stations to stop at and when. He knew which restaurants had the fastest food for the best quality based on proximity to the on-ramp. He knew when the local country radio station began to get fuzzy, and when to switch to the next station.

He had spent so much time driving across the state that the

journey had become automatic. Routine.

But this was no routine trip.

Ben was on his way to Indianapolis. And he had a deadline. His first grandchild would be born any minute.

A few months ago, Ben's daughter had been promoted, prompting a quick move to Indianapolis. Just in time to find an apartment and a delivery hospital.

Ben was out of state when he got the call that his daughter was going into labor. He jumped in his truck and drove. He knew the roads well. He knew the best route to take.

And he would not be late.

He couldn't be late.

"Next up, we have a heartwarming story about a dog who was lost for two years before returning home," the radio continued.

Ben turned the radio down.

He looked across the sun-drenched landscape, flat and unimposing. His mind drifted. It often did while he drove these roads. Today, his thoughts landed on his own daughter, his own experience as a first-time father.

He remembered that excitement. Calling his wife while on the road. Her telling him that it was time. The baby was coming. He jumped in his truck and sped through the night. He made it to the hospital a few hours after she was born.

Ben and his wife had planned on having another child. But it never happened.

Not because they couldn't. It was just that Ben was gone so much. His trucking routes started growing more frequent. He started traveling longer distances.

Then, suddenly, his daughter was five. She started kinder-garten when he was somewhere out on the highway hauling a shipment of grain to a processing plant somewhere in

California.

And then, she was ten. Ben missed her birthday. He was hauling steel beams from the plant in Iowa to a construction site in Pennsylvania. He called her from the motel to wish her a happy birthday, but she was already asleep by the time he called.

Ben's wife had filed for divorce before their daughter started middle school. He knew it was coming. He didn't fight it.

Then, his daughter started high school.

Ben was proud of his daughter's accomplishments. She joined student government, ran track, and played volleyball. And she got good grades.

But, as Ben continued his regular drives across the country, he came to a harsh realization: he wasn't responsible for his daughter's success. He wasn't around enough to have truly made an impact.

Still, he was proud of her.

She graduated from high school and went to college. After college, she got a job. Met a nice man and got married. She was living the American Dream.

Ben couldn't take credit for it, but he was proud of his daughter.

The silence began to make Ben nervous, so he decided to turn up the radio volume. The station he was listening to had shifted to static, so he changed the station. He was now in range for Indianapolis stations.

"*The Greenfield Sharks lost by a free throw last night, eliminating them from the playoffs, missing another window of opportunity to capitalize on their talent,*" the radio blared.

"I'm not missing this window of opportunity," Ben said. "Not this time."

As the sun began to dip beneath the horizon, Ben pressed the gas pedal harder and accelerated his truck.

Finally, he made it to Indianapolis. Finally, he made it to the exit. Finally, he would show up for his daughter. And for her daughter.

The Street

Iowa

Brian's fear of the outside world had begun to lessen in recent months. He watched the news less often. He had started going outside again. The virus, or public perception of it anyway, had caused him to close up, to rely on feelings of fight-or-flight anxiety. For the last year, Brian had remained indoors, afraid to venture much farther than his own front yard.

But, in some regard, the world had started to open up again. Stories on the evening news appeared less terror-inducing than they used to. Stories on social media were beginning to focus on other things, mostly unrelated to the virus.

It had taken weeks, but Brian had built up the courage to venture out of his house, out of his comfort zone. He decided to go to Main Street.

In a past life, Brian thrived on Main Street. He loved its vibrancy. The old brick buildings, repurposed to fit a new generation. The trendy restaurants, the swanky bars that served exotic cocktails, the boutiques, and the farmers markets. Everybody was always on Main Street.

Until the virus pushed everyone inside.

* * *

Brian tied his shoes, which felt unusually snug, a side effect of spending most of his time indoors and shoeless. He placed his mask on his face, put his hand sanitizer in his pocket, and walked out the door.

As he rounded the corner, he saw the street sign: Main Street. But while his excitement grew, so did his anxiety. He hadn't seen this many people in a long time. But he knew that he needed this social interaction. He craved it, but he also needed safety.

Brian stopped on the corner of Main and 12th. A feeling of joy began to creep into his mind. He stood on the street corner and allowed it to happen. He watched as people congregated at a food truck. Brian knew that everyone else must have craved this social interaction as much as he had. He knew that people would be kinder, gentler, after being cooped up for so long.

"Watch out, man," a teenager said as he walked by Brian, narrowly avoiding him.

"Sorry," Brian said. "Very sorry."

It wasn't a friendly interaction, but at least it was an interaction. Sparked by the prospect of connection, Brian began his walk down the sidewalk. Strolling along Main Street brought back a familiar ease, but Brian felt an unusual sense of anxiety grip him as he walked.

He held his head up, focusing on people. Brian smiled at a few groups who crossed his path, but his smile was hidden behind his mask. He had hoped that people understood that his eye contact was meant as a friendly greeting. But people didn't seem interested in his eye contact. In fact, he felt invisible.

As he walked, Brian looked closer at the groups he passed.

A group of five adults walked with each other. They all held phones in their hands. The screens absorbed their attention. Occasionally, one friend would show another friend his screen. But, mostly, they walked in silence, unaware of each other's existence.

Interesting, Brian thought. *Connected, but not to each other*.

He noticed a couple sitting on a bench. A man had headphones in his ears. He looked at his phone, enthralled with whatever his phone was displaying. A woman held her phone in her hand. Her thumb scrolled up. Her eyes followed the screen, unaware of her surroundings.

Couples are supposed to enjoy spending time with each other, Brian thought.

Brian looked around and noticed dozens of people who were focused on their phones. The devices seemed ingrained into the anatomy of each human, a new appendage, a new personality that required undivided attention. With all of this humanity surrounding them, with all of this potential for connection, these humans chose silence. They chose to allow algorithms to control their days.

He regretted his decision to step out of his door, out of his safe zone. The image of Main Street that he had cultivated in his mind was an image of an era that no longer existed. Masked, emotionless, disconnected people roamed a street that used to buzz with life and joy.

Brian stopped his walking pace and sat on an open bench. He forced his face into his palms. It was time to return home.

"Excuse me, sir," a kid said.

Brian lifted his face from his hands and looked at the kid.

"I think you dropped your wallet," the kid continued.

The kid handed an old wallet to Brian, who unfolded it to

make sure that his twenty dollar bill was still there. Seeing the green paper in the fold, Brian smiled.

"Thanks, kid," Brian said. "I really needed that honesty today."

The kid tilted her head and searched Brian's face for meaning. Brian smiled and waved the comment away.

"What's your name?" Brian asked.

The kid smiled. Three front teeth missing.

"Hope," the kid said.

Looking over Hope's shoulder, Brian saw a group of other kids, some masked, some not. All waiting for Hope to finish her conversation with the wallet-dropping man. Brian reached into his wallet and pulled out the twenty dollar bill. He handed it to the kid. Her eyes doubled in size.

"Go buy some ice cream for you and your friends," Brian said.

The kid squeezed the money in her hand as if it might float away. She struggled to contain the smile on her face.

"Thank you, sir," the kid said.

Brian nodded and waved her off. The kid scampered toward her friends. They all huddled around the twenty dollar bill. One kid removed his headphones. Another kid put her phone in her pocket. Their voices rang with enthusiasm, all connected by the good fortune that accompanied integrity. The kids dashed toward the ice cream shop a few blocks down Main Street.

As he stood from the bench, Brian felt lighter. He noticed the sun's warmth. As he began his walk home, he looked around at Main Street, buzzing with life, and smiled.

The Basketball

Kansas

Robby saw his defender commit, so he dished the basketball to Max running up the sideline. Robby's defender slid to cover the open man beneath the hoop, leaving Robby open at the three point line. Max dribbled in, and then passed to Robby. He caught it clean. No defenders in sight. He paused briefly and inhaled to calm himself, to tunnel his vision. Then, he sprung and flicked the ball into the air.

"And it's good from three!" the announcer shouted.

Robby pointed to Max, giving him visual credit for the assist. The buzzer echoed through the high school gym.

"Hawks win!" the announcer continued.

Robby jogged to the sideline. He put his fist into the center of the team circle. The rest of the team followed, bringing their attention closer to the center for the usual post-game speech from their captain.

"Great way to end the regular season, boys!" Robby shouted. "Let's celebrate the win tonight, but stay focused. Playoffs start next week."

He looked around the circle, making sure his teammates were on board. Satisfied with the nonverbal responses, he continued.

"Hawks on three," Robby said. "One, two, three!"

"Hawks!" the huddle shouted.

Robby jogged into the locker room and opened his locker. He changed out of his uniform and into his sweats and sweatshirt. His backpack, weighed down by his massive history book, felt heavy on his shoulders. But the pressure of tomorrow's test added extra weight.

"You played so well tonight, son," Robby's mom said as he jumped in the car.

Robby stared out the window. The crowd had already faded from the gym parking lot. The entryway lights were in the process of dimming.

"Thanks," Robby said.

His mom side-eyed him.

"Something wrong?" she asked.

Robby snapped his attention from the gym. He felt his backpack beneath his feet.

"No, nothing's wrong," Robby said, forcing his face into a smile.

Robby's mom shrugged and started the car. The drive home wasn't long. About ten minutes, mostly through backroads that cut through open fields.

Tonight, Robby wished the drive was longer.

The car pulled into the driveway and Robby hopped out and walked upstairs to his room. He tossed his backpack onto his bed. It was half-zipped, so his history book fell onto the floor. Robby walked over to pick it up.

"Why are *you* my toughest opponent tonight?" Robby asked, looking at his book.

He knew the consequences. If he didn't pass his U.S. history midterm tomorrow, he would earn a failing grade. And failing one class meant that he couldn't play basketball.

And the playoffs started in five days.

"Fail tomorrow's test," Robby said. "Miss the playoffs."

He pulled his study guide and notebook from his backpack and opened his textbook. He sorted through notes and scribbles and tried to find the answers to the practice test questions. The problem wasn't that he didn't understand. The problem was that this was too much information to fill one simple test. What if he spent all night studying about the Revolution, but most of the test was about the impact of slavery? What if he spent his time studying about slavery, but most of the test was about conflict with indigenous civilizations? What if he forgot the date of Nat Turner's rebellion? He might forget the name of the guy who said "Give me liberty or give me death."

There was too much content. And too little time.

Robby flipped through his study guide, scribbled furious notes, and read and reread sections of his textbook.

He woke up at sunrise with his textbook sprawled out next to him on the bed. Looking at the clock, he panicked.

"I overslept," he whispered.

Throwing on some clean clothes, he stuffed his school supplies into his backpack and jumped downstairs.

"Thought you'd never wake up," his mom said.

She smiled kindly. Robby grabbed an apple and ran to the car.

"I'm going to be late," Robby said, charging out the door.

His mom stood in the doorway with her car keys.

"Are you going to put on shoes?" she asked.

Robby threw his head back in frustration. He ran inside,

grabbed a pair of sneakers, and jumped in the passenger seat. His mom turned the car on and backed slowly out of the driveway.

As the car cruised down the street, Robby's attention drifted out the window. He watched the trees blur into a green cloud. His mind was focused on one thing: the test.

He knew what he had to do. Unfortunately, what he *had* to do was different from what he *should* do. Robby *should* have studied harder during the quarter. He *should* have gone to study sessions to get extra help on the smaller assignments. He *should* have put some actual effort into his homework. He *should* have paid more attention to his teacher in class instead of looking at Jennifer to see if she was looking at him so he could see if she liked him.

But he didn't do any of that. Now, he was faced with what he *had* to do.

He *had* to pass the test. And that meant that he *had* to cheat.

He didn't *want* to cheat. But he didn't have a choice. He had to play in the playoff game if his team had a chance at winning and moving on to the next round. Plus, college scouts would probably be there. If he didn't play because his grades weren't good enough, that would ruin his shot at getting an offer from a university team.

The car pulled into the high school's roundabout, snapping Robby's attention.

"You must be tired after last night's game," his mom said. "You're awfully quiet this morning."

"Sorry, Mom," Robby said. "I've just got a lot on my mind."

She smiled, her eyes creasing at the corners.

"Well, I'm so proud of you," she said. "Have a good day, sweetie."

Robby wanted to sink into his seat. Instead, he slunk out of the car. Joining the mass of students walking into the building, Robby ran through his half-formed scheme. He would try to sit by James, the smartest kid in school. One row behind him and one column to the left. That way, Robby could look over James's shoulder and make it look like he was looking at his own pencil. Hopefully, Nicholas would sit in front of him. Nicholas towered over Robby; he would make a good shield between the teacher and Robby's eyes.

Math class came and went. English flew by. Then Art was done. History was next.

Robby felt his pulse quicken as he strolled into the classroom. James wasn't in class yet, so Robby talked with another classmate without committing to a desk. Then, James walked in. Robby quickly snagged the desk behind him and to the left.

Perfect, he thought.

The bell rang. The teacher stood and quieted down the nervous test-takers. He distributed the paper packets to each desk. Robby held the test in his hand.

"Alright, class," the teacher said. "This test isn't about memorizing dates and the names of famous people. This test is about what you've gained from this unit. Read the directions, and begin."

Nervously, Robby read the directions.

What was the most impactful event in United States history?

Robby looked over James's shoulder. His paper shook in his hands. Robby's paper suddenly stilled.

I don't need you, Robby thought. *I got this.*

As Robby's pen flew across the page, his eyes never lifted.

* * *

The next day, the teacher handed back the essays. Robby knew he wouldn't get a high score, but he just needed to pass. As the teacher approached Robby's desk, he dropped the paper into Robby's hands.

"Good job," the teacher said. "Don't doubt yourself, Robby."

"B plus?" Robby whispered. "I did it."

As he put the test in his backpack, he could almost hear the sound of sneakers on the court, the sound of the scouts scribbling on their notepads, the sound of the crowd cheering as the clock wound down, the sound of the final buzzer.

The Camera

Even in such a serene environment, Emma felt fear somewhere deep within her senses. Her boots crunched the dried leaves as she stepped through the woods. She had left the trail a while ago. Everyone took the same photographs from the trail. She wanted something different. Something truly original.

The terrain was uneven, so she steadied herself by walking slower than her usual pace. She didn't want to drop her camera.

A golden leaf swirled alone on a tree branch. Emma approached the tree. She focused in on the leaf, lowered her shutter speed to slow the motion.

"Decent," Emma said, checking her camera screen.

She took another shot of the same leaf from a different angle, and then continued her walk through the woods. Emma wasn't exactly sure what she was trying to find. But she would know it when she saw it. Maybe she would come across a cliff with a sweeping view of the rolling hills, waves of orange and red leaves cascading over the land. Maybe she would see an owl perched in a tree. Maybe she would find an old, warped tree trunk that stood out, isolated in the wilderness.

No matter what she found, she wanted the images to tell a story.

As she continued her walk through the woods, Emma used her free hand to brush away the sparse undergrowth. The smell of dry autumn wafted through the chilled afternoon air.

Even if I don't find anything to shoot, Emma thought, *at least I'm out here.*

She had wanted to get out of the city for a while. The exhaust fumes from cars. The crowds of people elbowing their way to their next destination without a care for anyone but themselves. The subterranean pressure to succeed, that good was never good enough.

She decided to take the weekend off and drove into nature. Like she used to do. Before she started her career.

And being alone in nature was producing the desired impact. Emma felt the fog in her mind dissipate with every step, with every breath among the trees. She was beginning to see clearly again, removed from the tunnel vision of computer screens and phone screens and television and the high-pressure work environment that she had worked so hard to break into.

Clear vision.

And then she saw it.

The log cabin, uninhabited for years, sunk beneath the weight of leaves and rot. Its stone chimney was covered in moss. The door remained closed, but slightly unhinged. Birds and squirrels had created their own ecosystem around the cabin.

"What is this?" Emma said.

She looked around, reminding herself that she was completely alone. Or was she *convincing* herself?

Approaching the cabin carefully, Emma attempted to muffle

the crunch of leaves beneath her feet. She started with a wide shot of the cabin, framing the dead leaves and twisting trees with the shot. Then, she spun the lens and tightened the frame, focusing on the finer details of the cabin: the broken stained glass window, the rotting door frame, the warped wood, and the drooping shingles. The scene had so many possibilities. She didn't even stop to check her photos after she captured them. She could do that later. The lighting was too perfect. And the isolation was too nerve-tightening.

After walking around the cabin and taking hundreds of pictures, she finally stood back and looked at the cabin with her own eyes. The weight of the camera rested on her palm.

I found it, Emma thought. *The shot that no one else has gotten.*

Satisfied with her quest for the perfect photograph, she took one last look at the cabin and turned around, quickening her pace. As her feet crunched the dry leaves beneath her feet, she felt a sense of fear creep into her mind again. A sense that she wasn't alone.

* * *

The sun had set hours ago. Emma sat at her small desk against the window in her apartment. Cars buzzed six levels below, their headlights competing with stop lights for control of the night. She opened her computer and began to sift through her photos from her hike in the woods.

A few shots of decaying leaves against a tree.

These are alright, Emma thought.

She kept moving.

A wide-framed shot of the cabin.

Keeper, Emma thought.

She liked the way the shadows from the cabin looked on the leaf-covered ground.

A photo of drooped shingles on a moss-covered roof. She kept it.

And then she got to a photo of a broken stained glass window. She skipped over it. But then, she paused.

Oh no, she thought.

She quickly scrolled back to the photo of the stained glass window. The glass was green, red, and blue. It looked like it used to depict a scene of a river with trees around it. The cracks in the window spiderwebbed outward, but they all had a common starting point: a distinct hole in the center.

As her eyes narrowed on the hole in the glass, she thought she saw something. Emma placed the photo into her editing software. She brightened the photo and pulled up the shadows.

She stopped breathing.

There, in the shadowy recesses of the cabin's interior, was a face.

"I know that face," Emma said.

She pulled up her internet browser and began searching. After a few misguided search attempts, she finally found it. The article was two years old.

Notorious Jewel Thief Escapes Kentucky Prison.

She looked at the photo from the article. And then she looked at her photo from the cabin. And then she looked again at the article's picture.

"I found him," Emma said.

The Microphone

Louisiana

The crowd cheered wildly as Rashaad stepped back onto the stage. They had been shouting "encore" for over a minute. He wanted to jump back in front of the crowd after the first person yelled it, but he knew that he needed to wait, needed to let the suspense build.

A few hundred people filled the small auditorium. A small crowd. But, to Rashaad, it felt like he had sold out an arena. Throughout his entire set, the crowd had been singing along. And not just to one song, but to all six he performed.

People knew the words, memorized his lyrics.

People actually *cared* about what he had to say.

As he bounced back onto the stage for his encore, he clutched the microphone, wielding his weapon for change. The beat dropped. Bass reverberated throughout the compact stage. Rashaad threw his hands in the air and the crowd followed.

Inhaling deeply, Rashaad opened his lungs and spoke.

As I spit, you sit
Back, watch and observe.
I flick off ticks with toothpicks,
Nouns and verbs.

I bomb this with chopsticks,
Pick apart every word.

The crowd erupted. He spoke with such passion and such clarity that the crowd had to respond.

Sweat poured from his forehead. His dreadlocks swayed in front of his eyes, blocking the crowd from view. He swung his head, and his dreads swung with it. He breathed heavily, inhaling quickly between the few line breaks in his lyrics. He had trained for the physical demand of the stage, rapping while he sprinted on the treadmill. But the crowd-produced adrenaline took things to a new level.

As his final verse came to an end, he conjured up the energy to leave his show, to leave his audience filled with passion.

Louisiana stand up!
New Orleans stand up!
Louisiana stand up!
New Orleans stand up!

The crowd chorused the words back at him. Rashaad's mind filled with something that resembled pride with a dash of humility.

"Thank you, New Orleans!" Rashaad shouted into the microphone. "I'll see you again real soon!"

With that, Rashaad jogged off stage and disappeared from the audience's view. He handed the microphone to the stage manager. Grabbing a towel from his back pocket, he wiped the sweat from his forehead and moved down the short hallway into the dressing room. A metal folding chair awaited him. It wasn't a couch, but it would work for now.

"Yo, that was incredible!" Dizzy said. "The crowd knew all your lyrics."

He tossed a plastic water bottle to Rashaad.

"That was fun, man," Rashaad said, cracking open the lid. "That was only a few hundred people. I can't imagine what that feels like at a sold-out arena."

"You keep writing lyrics like that, spitting that heat, and you'll find out soon enough," Dizzy said.

"And you'll be right there with me, baby bro," Rashaad said. "We'll get there together."

They nodded to each other. The comfortable silence in the room communicated more than they could express. Sometimes, brothers didn't need to speak in order to understand.

The venue manager walked into the dressing room, breaking the calm. Rashaad stood and shook the manager's outstretched hand.

"That was some show," the manager said. "I've got your check right here."

Rashaad reached for it, restraining his eagerness. But, looking at the check, Rashaad's heart sank. It wasn't as much as he had hoped.

But it was something. And he knew the checks would get bigger if he kept at it.

"Thank you," Rashaad said.

"No," the manager said. "Thank you. This is one of the biggest crowds we've had. I know we're small. And new. But you brought the house down."

The manager smiled at Rashaad, and then smiled toward Dizzy.

"I'm still amazed at how many people show up for hip-hop concerts," the manager continued. "I don't understand why people like it so much. Maybe people are drawn to foul language and songs without much actual music."

Rashaad looked at Dizzy. Neither of them changed their

expressions, but they shared an understanding. And now they were going to have to do something about it.

Why didn't this guy just keep his damn mouth shut. Rashaad thought.

"The lyrics speak to people, man," Dizzy said, unable to hold himself back. "These lyrics are diverse and challenging and complex and poetic. They tell stories and uplift people's spirits and connect with people's hearts to let them know that someone else understands their struggle, that someone else cares."

The manager smiled meekly, a smile that showed his disagreement.

"I just mean that hip-hop isn't really *music*," the manager said. "It's just beats and pieces of music from actual musicians."

Rashaad couldn't help himself. He had to jump in.

"Hip-hop is full of so much music. And the music behind the lyrics comes from centuries of African and African-American heritage," Rashaad said. "Drum beats were used as forms of communication. Jazz was creativity configured from oppression. And neighborhoods with limited access to other instruments created instruments of their own from record scratches and sampling. Fusing all of those elements together, you could actually argue that hip-hop is the *most* musical genre."

"That all sounds nice," the manager said, "but you can't even understand rappers. And, even when you can, all they talk about is nasty, violent stuff."

"Must be terrible to have to work a little harder to understand the meaning of something," Dizzy said. "Rappers talk about real life. Their struggles, their successes in the face of oppression, real emotions, real stories. Plus, we not speaking *to you*. We speak *for us*."

Rashaad smirked at his brother.

"And you don't seem to mind taking your cut from a hip-hop artist's concert," Rashaad said.

The manager's face reddened. He had pigeonholed himself, not considering how one flippant comment could evoke so much emotion. He looked to Dizzy, and then to Rashaad. He offered a kind smile, something that resembled an apology. Maybe reconciliation.

"You're welcome to stick around as long as you want," the manager said.

He nodded and scurried out of the room, closing the door behind him.

Dizzy stood and picked up his backpack. Rashaad walked over to the table and grabbed his duffel bag. As they walked down the short hallway, Rashaad could still hear the remnants of the crowd.

Outside the venue, humidity stuck to Rashaad's shirt.

"Let's jump back on the tour bus," Rashaad said.

Their tour bus was a small van. Calling it a tour bus was more than a stretch, but it gave them amusement. It made them feel official.

Dizzy turned the key and backed the van up, dodging the dumpsters. The engine revved as the van pulled onto the street. The air was black, pierced only by a few streetlights. Rashaad turned on the stereo. A new beat without lyrics echoed through the car.

Rashaad pulled a notebook from his backpack. He flipped through it, passing pages and pages of rhymes and lines and lyrics. Some good. Some in progress.

He turned to a blank page and started scribbling.

Sometime I might
Turn a blind eye
To the margins of the page,
The same place I reside.
With too much focus on the chase,
Counting dollars every day,
I will not give into temptation
To leave community behind.
I make a vow right here and now
To always speak for all my people,
Prioritizing voiceless voices
Over greed and other evils.

The lyrics were unpolished, but he needed to get them out of his mind. He needed to get them on paper. Soon enough, he would make them exist on record.

He closed his notebook and put it back in his backpack. He leaned against the window and let his eyes close. The red and white lights of passing cars flickered against his eyelids.

The Writer

Maine

Mary watched the waves roll in from far out in the ocean. Each wave built momentum, churning somewhere far below the surface, before crashing into the rocks, sending salty spray in the air. Mary had been watching the waves since sunrise. She hoped to draw inspiration from the ocean, but she hadn't moved in hours. Her pen stayed still. Her paper blank. Her novel unfinished.

Even though her novel writing process was moving slower than she wanted, her mind still fired with thought. As she watched the waves crash down, she thought about her own momentum as a writer.

When she was younger, when her hair was more brown than gray, she had stamina. She wrote like she had something to prove. And she had proven it.

Now, she wrote as if she had nothing left to say.

But she did. Or, she wanted to, anyway.

Stacks of unfinished manuscripts piled on her desk in the corner of her cottage. Over the years, Mary had written, and rewritten, and moved to another story. Maybe those stories would have been good, but her motivation waned, and so did her attention to the process.

Looking at her own reflection in the window, she noticed her deep wrinkles, the dark bags beneath her eyes, the wisps of her gray hair. Realistically, she knew that she only had one good novel left in her.

As the sun rose to eye level, Mary couldn't handle the harsh light anymore, so she stood and walked to the kitchen to make tea. The tea kettle whistled, a shrill sound that echoed through the empty house.

The sound sparked an idea in her mind, an idea reminding her that she had no idea what to write about. Historical fiction interested her. She always enjoyed reading a good historical fiction story. But, at this point in her life, she had lived through so much history that it wouldn't qualify as fiction. Maybe she could count that as a memoir? But she hadn't considered her life interesting enough to write a memoir. She hadn't lived through a wartime event, or experienced a significant hardship, or become completely famous. No one would care about her insignificance. And she didn't want to recycle the types of books that she had written as a younger author. Her perspective had changed. Her priorities had shifted.

The waves calmed. Fewer and fewer rolled and crashed into the rocks. Mary finished her tea.

Perhaps it was a jolt of caffeine. Or the energy from direct sunlight. Whatever it was, Mary stood. She put on her shoes and grabbed her car keys and drove into town.

She hadn't been to town in a while. It proved overwhelming at times. New high rises and trendy restaurants and coffee shops seemed to appear overnight. More people roamed the narrow sidewalks than they used to. And she wasn't as sure-footed as she used to be.

Mary parked her car along a side street. The old car's long body creaked into its parallel parking spot between two electric vehicles. Mary got out of her car and locked it. She double-checked that her windows were rolled up. The overcast sky could rain any minute.

She walked down the sidewalk, navigating the uneven concrete that had cracked and shifted over time, its moss made slick by the ocean mist.

Mary walked by an old restaurant that had been there since she was a kid. She remembered going to it with her mother on weekends in the summer. The owner hadn't painted the sign in decades. It hung from a metal chain, rusted by salt water and the passage of time.

An old man with a gray beard averted his eyes as he passed Mary and entered the restaurant. He looked like he went there every day.

Passing the restaurant, Mary pulled her sweater tight over her chin to ward off the chill that blew in from the ocean. She walked by a shop that sold trinkets and antiques and sea-themed Americana. She passed a coffee shop that wasn't there last time she came to town. She passed the tavern and a few office buildings that seemed occupied by a growing influx of realtors.

And then she saw another restaurant. It seemed new. Or newer. But not trendy or pretentious. An unassuming storefront with enough upkeep to show potential customers that the owner cared.

A bell above the door chimed as Mary entered. A young host dressed in a vest and a bowtie greeted her. He looked like he was still in high school.

"Welcome to The Seashell," the host said. "Table for one?"

Mary smiled kindly and nodded. The host grabbed a menu and led her to the back of the restaurant. The window overlooked the ocean, which extended endlessly until it disappeared into the fog.

"Can I start you off with something to drink?" a server asked.

"Just a hot tea, please," Mary said.

The host nodded and disappeared to get the tea.

A college football game played on an old television that hung in the corner of the room. Some customers watched it passively, but the waves out the window commanded more attention. Mary grabbed a piece of bread from the middle of her table. It felt fresh and softened in her hand.

The server returned and placed a small pot of tea on the table. He lifted the pot and poured some steaming tea into Mary's cup. She thanked him. As he walked away, she wondered if he was about her grandchildren's age. She hadn't heard from them in months. They lived in the city, a long drive down the coast from Mary's cabin. She usually saw them on Christmas and sometimes on Thanksgiving. Maybe the occasional summer trip. They rolled into town and rolled out again with a distinct rhythm.

Mary looked around the restaurant. Most tables were occupied, but no one seemed in a hurry. They were all just existing, enjoying being present.

She remembered a time when she would have known everyone in a restaurant like this, back when the town was even smaller. Back when she was younger and more involved. Back before everyone left, replaced by new faces. But she figured that something like that happened to everyone who stuck around their hometown long enough. The face that a child views as familiar wasn't always that community staple.

People rolled into town, crashed for a while, and then rolled out again, leaving some trace of its existence there before another wave rolled in.

As Mary thought about her town during her time with her own familiar faces, she reached for her purse and grabbed her notebook and pen. She started writing.

The Daughter

Maryland

The wooden table had been in Lindsay's family as long as she could remember. She had basically memorized all the grooves in the wood. Her chair, the chair against the wall side of the dining room, was too short on the front left leg, making it perfect for rocking.

"He's such a nice guy," Mom said.

"A real good head on his shoulders," Dad said.

Lindsay looked across the table and watched her sister's reaction.

"Yeah," Rachel said. "I like him a lot."

Dad smiled and looked at Lindsay.

"You see, Lindsay," Dad said, "in a few years, maybe you'll meet a guy like Barton and get ready to settle down like your big sister."

Lindsay forced a smile. The last thing she wanted to think about was settling down with a mediocre guy like Barton. Besides, she had other things to worry about. Like figuring how to raise enough money for the music festival she wanted to go to over Spring Break with her college roommate.

Plus, she was nothing like her sister. Rachel had always been a perfect student, on student council and homecoming queen and all that. Lindsay just liked to go with the flow. She had friends. Lots of them. But she liked to step out of her comfort zone to find her growth. Lindsay was pretty sure that Rachel had never even left the state.

But Barton had just left the family dinner table to go back to his own house with his own family behind his own private gate in his own isolated neighborhood. And if that's what Rachel wanted, then she could have it.

But Lindsay wanted more.

"You've dated Barton since your sophomore year in college," Dad said. "And you've been out of college for a year. Have you two talked about the next step?"

"Marriage?" Lindsay blurted.

She felt her face redden. Rachel cast a disapproving glance across the table.

"We actually have talked about the idea of getting married," Rachel said. "Barton is ready."

"How do you feel about it?" Dad asked.

Rachel lowered her eyes.

"He's a great guy," Rachel said. "I'm just not ready. There are other things I want to do first."

"Well, honey," Dad said. "Barton comes from an impressive family. He has a steady job at the investment firm that already makes him a lot of money. With a setup like that, you might not even have to work. You could leave your job at the bank."

Rachel looked up from the table. She felt her eyes drift toward Lindsay, worried about her rebellious sister's response. Rachel had always envied Lindsay's carefree spirit, her confidence to be who she wanted, not who her parents wanted.

But, instead of disapproval, Lindsay's eyes spoke something

else, something that resembled empathy.

Lindsay always assumed that her sister projected her true self. But here, Lindsay saw something else in her sister. Something familiar.

"Barton is a great guy," Rachel said, her voice meek.

Dad smiled across the table to Mom.

"Well, that settles it," Dad said. "Time for Barton to put a ring on that finger."

"We need grandkids running around here as soon as possible," Mom added.

Lindsay's eyes widened. She looked at Rachel, whose eyes still hadn't left the floor.

As dinner ended, Lindsay scooped up her plate and took it to the kitchen. She returned and grabbed Rachel's plate. She wanted Rachel to leave the dinner table as soon as she could. The discomfort was palpable, but only the sisters felt it.

Rachel slunk away from the table and climbed the stairs to her room. Well, her *old* room. She lived in an apartment across town, but she was staying at her family's house for the holidays since her sister came home from college. Rachel's room hadn't changed much since she was in high school. Ribbons and awards and trophies adorned her shelves. Old high school textbooks that she never got rid of. It was clean, rigid, and sterile. Unlike Lindsay's room, with its band posters and edgy art prints and black-and-white photographs.

Rachel heard Lindsay's loud footsteps coming up the stairs. She expected Lindsay to go into her room and turn on some music, maybe even watch a show. Instead, the footprints kept moving into Rachel's room.

"Hey, Rach," Lindsay said, popping her head into the doorframe. "Can I come in?

Rachel grabbed a pillow and squeezed it for comfort.

"Of course," Rachel said.

Lindsay sat cross-legged on the floor.

"I know you're getting a lot of pressure from Mom and Dad about getting married and all that," Lindsay said.

Rachel's eyebrows perked.

"Oh, no," Rachel said. "It's not pressure. It's what I should be doing. It's the natural next step."

Lindsay felt adrenaline course through her body.

"But it's not the natural next step," Lindsay said. "There is no natural next step."

"But it's what Mom and Dad expect," Rachel said.

"Who cares what they expect?" Lindsay said. "It's not their life. It's yours. You should do what you want to do. If marrying Barton and leaving your job to stay at home with three kids behind a white picket fence is what you want to do, then do it. But if it's not, then don't."

Rachel buried her face in the pillow. As she spoke, her voice muffled.

"It's not what I want to do," Rachel said. "Barton is a nice guy, but I don't want to get married and settle down yet. I want a job. I went to college for a reason. I want to see the world. I don't want to be trapped behind a white picket fence in the suburbs until I die."

Lindsay raised an eyebrow. She had never heard this type of honesty from her older sister before.

"But how do I do that when Mom and Dad expect something else?" Rachel asked. "How do you have the courage to do what you want, to be who you want? You just walk around like nothing bothers you, like you don't care what anyone else thinks. I envy you for that."

"It's not as easy as it looks," Lindsay said. "I actually care a lot about what certain people think. Mom. Dad. And mostly you."

Rachel raised her head from the pillow and tilted her head as she looked at her sister.

"You care what I think?" she asked.

"Of course I do," Lindsay said.

Rachel and Lindsay smiled at each other, a smile that held so much meaning that no one except the sisters could understand.

"Well, if I'm going to live how I want, then I'm going to need your help," Rachel said.

"Of course, Rach," Lindsay said. "What do you need?"

Rachel looked around to make sure her parents weren't listening.

"I've never left the East Coast," Rachel said. "I figure that now is the best time to travel the world."

"Barton wants to leave his job at the investment firm and travel the world?" Lindsay asked.

"Nope," Rachel said. "It's time for me to figure out who I am on my own."

Lindsay smiled and stood and hugged her sister. And, as they sat on Rachel's bed, they began looking for flights.

The Rich Uncle

Massachusetts

Mr. Strauss walked down his grand staircase into the foyer. He held the wooden railing, sliding his slippered feet along the cool marble stairs. He looked up at the golden chandelier. Its crystals bounced light around the open room.

The doorbell rang again and an elongated chime echoed through the house. Mr. Strauss had expected his butler to answer the door, but he seemed to be engaged in more pressing matters.

Pausing at the last step, Mr. Strauss inhaled, and then exhaled deeply, calming himself for the impending shift of environment. He walked to the old oak door and opened it. His nephew stood in the doorway. His hair curled out beneath his backwards baseball cap. He wore a soccer jersey and jeans. And his face epitomized the spirit of youthful rebellion.

A generation of freeloaders with no respect for hard work, Mr. Strauss thought.

"Hey, Uncle Hank!" Sammy said.

"Hello, Samuel," Mr. Strauss said. "Welcome to my estate."

Sammy tightened his backpack straps and walked inside. He stood in the foyer and looked up.

"Uncle, you're living in luxury," Sammy said. "I'm going to enjoy staying here."

Mr. Strauss frowned.

"I've earned the privilege of living in luxury," Mr. Strauss said. "I've worked extremely hard for my wealth by pulling myself up by my bootstraps. Something your mother and father wouldn't know much about."

Sammy wandered through the foyer and looked at the ornate vases and statues that decorated the otherwise cold interior.

"Well, with my dad working double shifts at the cannery, and my mom teaching and getting her master's, I'd say they're working harder than most people," Sammy said.

Mr. Strauss rolled his eyes.

"If they were really working hard," Mr. Strauss said, "then they wouldn't need to send you here for the summer."

Sammy smiled.

"If they had married into a wealthy family like you," Sammy said, "then you and I wouldn't get to spend so much quality time together."

Sammy's smile never wavered, nor did his innocent tone, but the truth of his youthful words stung Mr. Strauss.

Footsteps echoed down the hallway. The butler appeared from the dark corridor and approached Mr. Strauss.

"The deal is done," the butler whispered.

He turned his attention to Sammy.

"Welcome to the estate," the butler said. "I'll take your bag. You can follow me upstairs to your quarters."

"I can carry my own bag, but thank you," Sammy said.

He looked over at his uncle.

"Man, you guys talk real fancy around here."

Mr. Strauss smirked.

"Yes, I suppose we do speak with a certain refinement that you're not accustomed to."

Sammy had a lot that he wanted to say, but he held his thoughts. Instead, he turned and followed the butler up the grand staircase and walked down the hallway. Lit only by a few antique-looking wall lamps, the butler's footsteps echoed through the otherwise silent mansion.

The butler opened the door to a bedroom that was larger than Sammy's entire apartment in Boston.

"May I get you anything before I retire?" the butler asked.

"No thanks," Sammy said. "But I appreciate the offer."

The butler nodded and disappeared down the dark hallway. Sammy tossed his backpack onto a chair and flopped down on the bed.

I can't believe I have to spend the whole summer up here on Mansion Row, Sammy thought.

He would rather spend his summer at home in his neighborhood. His neighborhood wasn't glamorous. But he had friends. He had a routine. He knew his neighbors and the owner of the corner store and the sound of the street corner and the smell from the unnamed market that sold fish sandwiches. But his parents wanted Sammy to spend the summer with their uncle so they could work more without him left unsupervised. Besides, Mr. Strauss lost his wife a few years ago and had been quite reclusive since her passing. And they figured it would be a chance for Sammy to network with important figures in high society. Looking at the row of mansions that lined the ocean, Sammy believed that these families had social standing. They probably had last names that colleges and institutes were named after.

Already bored, Sammy decided to explore the mansion. He

wandered through the dark corridors. Their wooden walls smelled old and musty. Sammy weaved into another hallway, passing closed doors with no light emitting from beneath them.

As he turned the corner near the back of the mansion, Sammy noticed a thin stairway. It wasn't the grand staircase. No. This one was meant to remain unnoticed. Sammy walked down it slowly. Each step creaked beneath his feet. The stairwell rounded, creating a blind corner.

Sammy heard low voices. He slowed his walk, taking care to step on the outer edges of each step to reduce his noise.

Then, the voices grew just loud enough for Sammy to discern their meaning.

"How dare they reduce my share of the trust fund," Mr. Strauss said. "She was my wife. I have a right to that money."

"The family lawyers claim that you don't," the butler said. "They claim that, because the family earned that wealth over the course of a century before you came into the picture, that you don't have any right to the family fortune."

There was a pause. Sammy inched closer to the stairway's opening to hear what came next.

"And they claim that, since she was your third wife, that you were only after her money," the butler continued.

Sammy slapped his hand over his mouth to contain his laughter.

"If they take that money," Mr. Strauss said, "I'm ruined."

Unable to control his impulse, Sammy walked down the stairs. He emerged in an ornate office. Bookshelves lined with hardcovers that had likely never been read. A massive globe rested in a stand on the floor.

"I thought you earned all your money through hard work

and merit," Sammy said.

Mr. Strauss snapped his head around and saw Sammy standing in the doorway.

"What are you doing in here?" Mr. Strauss said. "This is *my* office."

Sammy smirked.

"Seems like it won't be for long," he said.

Mr. Strauss's eyes bulged from his reddening face.

"If you lose your wife's trust fund," Sammy continued, "I'm sure my dad could get you a job at the cannery."

The butler resisted the urge to laugh.

"It's hard work though," Sammy said. "It might take you some time to get used to that."

The Factory

Michigan

Light snow fell. It wasn't late, but the sky was dark. Winter seemed to come earlier and earlier every year. Jack tucked his chin into his coat collar to ward off the chill. He felt the cold in his knees, a credit to his age and his years of service at the automotive assembly factory. Jack walked by rows of tightly packed homes lined with rusted chain link fences, but he kept his eyes low. Cracks spiderwebbed through the concrete sidewalk.

"Hey, Jack!" a familiar voice shouted.

Jack looked up and squinted through the darkness. A streetlight shined orange beams through the snow onto a porch stoop.

"Cordell?" Jack asked.

"And who else do you think would be yelling at you from my porch?" Cordell said.

Jack smirked and straightened his beard. The black-and-gray strands felt coarse against his rough hands.

"Come on up and have a drink, brotha," Cordell said.

Jack walked closer to the porch. He stopped at the low chain link fence and put his hands on the metal gate.

"I'd better not," Jack said. "I've got to get home to Marcy."

Cordell laughed and slapped his knee.

"Stop lying," Cordell said. "We both know you don't have no place to be on a Thursday night. Marcy will be fine on her own for a little while. In fact, she'll probably enjoy the extra time to watch her shows without you jabbering away."

Jack thought about his wife. They'd been married for over three decades. And Cordell was right. She probably would enjoy a few more minutes of peace and solitude.

He smiled and unlatched the gate. It creaked open, burdened by years of rust and snow and time and use.

"Take a seat," Cordell said.

Jack sat on a middle step, one step below Cordell. The steps were wooden and warped. Cordell reached onto the stoop and grabbed a beer can and handed it to Jack.

"Thanks," Jack said.

They sat in silence. The orange streetlight caught light snowflakes as they fell. In the distance, smokestacks from the factory stood as silhouettes. Smoke and steam used to puff from the brick tower, but the factory had fallen into disrepair, unused for three years.

"Haven't seen you in a minute," Cordell said. "What's new?"

Jack sipped his beer and let out an audible exhale.

"Just trying to stay out of trouble," Jack said. "With the kids all moved out on their own, and without the factory to keep me busy, I've been spending a lot of time at the church."

Cordell shook his head and slapped his knee.

"Man, how things have changed," he said. "Remember when we first started at the factory, and we used to stop at the bar almost every night after our shift?"

"Sure do," Jack said. "We'd catch a football game, or watch

the Pistons. Throw down a few tall ones and then walk home."

"We used to throw quarters in the jukebox and play that Motown sound all through that old bar," Cordell said.

Jack laughed and took another drink.

"I miss those days, man," Cordell said.

"Me too," Jack said. "Too bad we'll never get them back."

They both sat in silence and looked at the factory tower in the distance.

"Especially now that the factory closed down," Cordell said. "But hey. At least you got to stick around for another few months after they laid me off."

"The place really started to crumble after you left," Jack said. "They started making us do double shifts for half the wage to make up for it."

Cordell shook his head and took a drink. He looked toward the factory. One of these days, he expected to see a smoke stack crumble to the ground.

"Back in high school, we couldn't wait to graduate and start working at the factory," Jack said. "We couldn't wait to piece together brand new cars and ride through the city, flaunting our money."

"Riding in four-doors that *we* built, listening to Motown from our stereos," Cordell said. "Riding with the windows down in the summer."

"And the heat turned all the way up in the winter," Jack added.

Jack remembered those days fondly, his memories shaded in a golden hue. He remembered leaving the factory every day after a ten-hour shift, sweaty and covered in smoke and steam. He walked by the brick wall, strong and sturdy. He sat in his car, rolled down the window and shouted to Cordell in the car next to him. They drove in a line down the main drag. At a stoplight, Jack's engine revved and his chest swelled with pride at the power he helped to create. Lighting a cigarette, he nodded to the neighbors on the corner, the ones who worked, but not in the factories.

He pulled his car against the curb and opened his door. He sat on the hood of the car, smiling at people who passed. When enough of his friends got there, he walked into the bar with Cordell and they stayed until way too late, usually walking home if they had too much. And he always showed up to work on time the next day.

"We'll never get those days back," Jack said. "Our town is changing."

Cordell nodded and took another drink.

"We lost that spirit," Jack continued. "That attitude that you can do it yourself, no matter what anyone else thinks about us."

Cordell exhaled as he looked into the night sky, a sky that was dark, yet simultaneously illuminated by the aura of the city.

"Maybe it's not lost," Cordell said. "Maybe it's still out there somewhere, taking a different form, a form that our old eyes can't see. But it's out there."

Jack finished his beer and set the can down on the step. He stood slowly, his knees rusted.

"I sure hope it's out there somewhere," Jack said.

He turned and shook Cordell's hand.

"Thanks for the drink," Jack said.

"Thanks for stopping," Cordell said. "Just like the good old days."

Jack smiled. Backlit by the streetlight, his breath enveloped his beard.

"The good old days are gone, my friend," Jack said. "But maybe the present will be just as good."

He strolled up to the metal gate, latching it behind him as he left the yard. Jack waved one final time to Cordell before disappearing into the cold shadows.

"It's not lost," Cordell said to himself. "I know it's still out there."

The Mall

Minnesota

Cars packed the parking lot. Janet wove her minivan up and down each row, scouring the shadows of the undercover parking garage for a space. She thought she saw a spot close to an entrance, but a motorcycle occupied it. She kept driving until she found a spot near the edge of the lot.

She stopped the car and her husband got out, squeezing himself between the minivan and the car next to it. All three kids exited the car, mostly by their own power. Janet and her family scurried through the parking lot, dodging carloads of rabid shoppers.

"Alright, kids," Janet shouted. "Stick together. If anyone gets lost, meet by the ice skating rink in an hour."

The automatic doors spread open and the family entered the mall.

Immediately, the smell of the food court wafted toward them. Janet could hardly contain her urge to purchase a cinnamon roll.

"I'm going to look at video games!" Vinny shouted.

He darted off down the walkway and scampered up the escalator.

"I'm going with him!" Brody yelled.

He followed in his older brother's wake, weaving through the crowd before jumping onto the escalator.

"Can we go look at toys?" Jen asked.

She looked up at her mom with wide eyes, her face simultaneously pouting and smiling.

"Of course we can," Janet said. "But first, let's get cinnamon rolls."

They walked to the cinnamon roll stand at the food court and ordered three giant rolls. Prices were inflated because it was the mall, but Janet didn't mind. She paid with her credit card.

Their open table overlooked the ice rink. Janet and her husband wolfed down their rolls and waited while Jen picked at hers. Janet's husband grew impatient, so he went to a fast food stand and bought two massive sodas. Janet gulped hers down. Her husband dug into his ice with a straw to see if he could salvage any more sugary fizz. Jen was done with her roll after a few bites.

"It's alright, dear," Janet said. "Just throw it in the garbage and we'll keep shopping."

They stood and walked down the path, passing store after store after store. Most windows had flashy signs that advertised once-in-a-lifetime prices and seasonal sales.

"Now, look at this," Janet said. "Three dresses for the price of two. We can't pass this up."

"But you have so many dresses already, and you don't even wear most of them," Jen said.

"But this deal is too good to miss," Janet said.

She walked in and paid for three expensive dresses, putting the total cost on her credit card. Even though she couldn't afford it now, she'd pay for it later, with just a little extra in interest. They left the store and continued on through the hoards of people with piles of shopping bags in their arms, laughing and stressing.

"Let's go find your brothers," Janet said.

They stepped onto the escalator and allowed its mechanical magic to propel them upward to the second level of the mall. Passing store after store that sold thing after thing, they eventually came to the video game shop. Vinny and Brody stood near the center of the store, each with two video games in their hands.

"Mom!" Brody shouted. "Buy these for us!"

Youthful energy exuded through his voice.

"Of course I can, dear," Janet said.

The brothers scampered to the front desk and set their games on the counter. As the cashier scanned the games, Janet saw the prices flash on the screen. Her eyes widened. Her credit card felt heavy in her hands.

But she paid anyway.

"Mom," Jen said. "Can we go to the toy store now?"

Janet concealed her internal burden with a smile.

"Yes, dear," she said. "Let's round up the boys and we'll go find the toy store."

Janet corralled her sons and yanked them from the video game store. Jen followed, quickening her little steps to keep up. They passed group after group, family after family carrying bags and bags. Jen looked at her mom, arms loaded with bags, and realized that she belonged to one of those groups.

As the toy store approached, Jen felt guilt sprinkle into her mind. She looked around the store. Each aisle was filled with fun games and dolls and playsets and gadgets. She wanted all of them. But she needed none of them.

"What do you want to get, dear?" Janet asked.

Jen looked at her brothers, and then at her dad, and then back to her mom.

"Nothing," Jen said.

Janet eyed Jen, searching her face for her daughter's true intention.

"Why not?" Janet asked. "Are these toys not good enough for you?"

Jen smiled and began to leave the store.

"These toys look fun," Jen said. "But I don't actually need anything."

Her brothers looked at her with repulsion. They could not understand how a kid could walk into a toy store with an open invitation and crave nothing.

But Jen did crave things. She wanted every toy in the store. She wanted the gadgets and dolls and cars and bats and playsets. But she didn't need them. She didn't feel a compulsion to acquire stuff.

For once, she simply wanted to be.

"Can we get something?" Vinny shouted.

"Of course you can," Janet said.

Jen smiled and walked out of the store. She found an empty bench that overlooked the center of the mall. She sat quietly, watching families dash through the mall as they searched for sales and deals on things that were nothing more than that. Things.

The Thief

Mississippi

The school bell rang. Sixth graders sprang from their seats and scrambled out the door. Mya grabbed her homework folder and slid it into her backpack. She stood and hustled out of the classroom before her teacher could talk to her. There was something about a teacher's look that always made her feel like she was in trouble.

In the hallway, she blended in with all the other kids dashing from their lockers to their friends to the exit.

And that was fine with her.

Especially today.

"What's good, Mya?" Gabby said. "You got plans after school?"

Mya's eyes shifted from Gabby to the exit.

"Yeah, kind of," Mya said.

"You want to go ride bikes with us later?" Gabby asked.

Mya clutched the straps on her backpack.

"Maybe," Mya said. "If I have time."

Gabby eyed Mya. She looked like she might press the issue, but a boy bumped into her, drawing her attention away.

"Watch out, Brian," Gabby said.

"It was an accident," Brian said.

Gabby hit him in the arm. He grabbed his shoulder dramatically and threw a smirk toward Gabby, an expression that she returned.

"Alright, Mya," Gabby said. "Hit me up if you want to ride bikes later."

Mya nodded, thankful to be out of the conversation. She liked Gabby. They had been friends since second grade. But today was not the day for questions.

Mya walked out of the school building and walked along the concrete path to the sidewalk. She walked quickly. She had a deadline. Students crowded the street corners, informal street reporters talking about their after school plans and the events of the day. A few kids waved to Mya. She waved back, but continued her pace and direction.

She took a left down a back alley and weaved around the dumpsters until she emerged onto a side street. She paused and leaned against a brick wall beneath the neon sign for Mike's Market. This was the third-closest corner store from school, so it usually didn't attract much of a crowd. And that's why she chose it.

Time was running short. The elementary school would get out in a few minutes, and then the market would be flooded with kids. And their parents.

Even though the sun was out, Mya put her sweatshirt on and pulled the hood up around her ears. She wanted to seem anonymous, but not suspicious. Looking down the brick wall, she saw a customer leave the corner store. Now was her chance. Inhaling deeply to calm her nerves, she forced herself to stroll along the sidewalk and open the door.

The bell above the entrance rang as she entered, startling her

106

already-accelerating heartbeat. The old man at the counter was busy organizing magazines.

"Hey there," he said, without lifting his gaze from the magazines.

Mya wanted to nod. She wanted to keep her voice undetected, but she knew that silence could give away her plan.

"Hi," Mya said.

She turned down the second aisle, quickly escaping the old man's view. She walked by the chips, pretending to be interested in the newest flavors that always seemed to taste just like the old flavors.

But she wasn't here for chips. She continued through the aisle and rounded the corner by the cold drinks before turning down the candy aisle.

This was it.

Mya spotted the gummy candies, the sour candies, and the peanut-filled candies. Personally, she would have gone for the caramel-filled squares, but she wasn't here for herself.

As her eyes scanned the display, she saw it: the classic, massive chocolate bar. The one wrapped in iconic foil. The name brand. The one that signified high-quality, chocolatey excellence.

Mya snuck a glance down the aisle. She saw the top of the old man's bald head, still engaged in magazine organization. She double-checked the other direct, ensuring that she was still the only customer in the store. After assessing the situation, she knew that now was the time. Feeling herself shrink, she snatched the chocolate bar and put it in her sweatshirt pocket.

Guilt tore away at her nerves immediately. She nearly lost her ability to control her limbs. But she forced her legs to move. She walked toward the back of the store, casually making her way through the next aisle. After pretending to reexamine the chips, she sped up her pace and walked toward the door.

Her heart raced. She could feel the heat from the sun shining through the glass window. She was almost free. Mya reached out her hand and grabbed the door handle.

The old man never looked up.

"Hold it right there, young lady," the old man said.

His voice was assertive, yet calm. He moved away from the magazines and walked slowly around the counter.

"You weren't thinking of walking out of her without paying for that chocolate bar in your pocket, were you?" the old man asked.

Mya looked at him. She wondered how he could have possibly seen her put the candy bar in her pocket. Her glare proved too long. She couldn't respond.

"I'll bet you're wondering how I knew," the old man said. "You see, that sign outside says Mike's Market. I'm Mike. This is my market."

Mya's eyes widened.

"I've been doing this for decades," Mike said. "I've seen that look hundreds of times."

Mya tried to shake any form of expression off of her face.

"What look?" Mya said. "I don't have a look."

Mike smiled. His eyes crinkled around the edges.

"It's the look of desperation," Mike said. "Let me guess. You're helping someone out?"

Mya felt her shield dissipate. She frowned and nodded her head.

"Who are you helping out?" Mike asked.

"My little brother," she said. "He's in third grade. He walks by this store every day after school. And all the kids come in

108

and get candy. And then they stand outside and talk about their candy. But my little brother, he can't buy candy. And so everyone makes fun of him."

She paused to catch her breath.

"He'll walk by here any minute," Mya continued. "I thought it would be nice if I could hand him a candy bar today. That way, kids would stop picking on him."

Mya felt her eyes well with tears. She inhaled, forcing her tears to remain small pools in her eyes.

"I don't want him to feel the way I feel," she said.

Mike frowned. He crossed his arms, and then shifted his frown into a scowl. He wanted to ask why her little brother couldn't buy candy, but he already knew the answer. And he didn't want to embarrass Mya by asking.

"I'll tell you what, young lady," Mike said. "I'll give you that candy bar. You give it to your brother. And, while you're at it, go back there and pick out another one for yourself."

Mya let the tears fall from her eyes. As they trickled down her face, her smile caught them.

She didn't thank Mike. She couldn't say anything. But Mike knew. He could see it in her face.

Walking quickly to the candy aisle, Mya picked out a small pack of caramel-filled rolls. She stopped at the front aisle and smiled at Mike. She opened her mouth to speak, but no words came out.

"I know," Mike said.

Mya walked out of the store. She removed her sweatshirt and stuffed it in her backpack. As she was putting her backpack on her shoulders, she heard the shouts and laughs of elementary school kids walking around the corner. A few kids walked by her and sprang into Mike's Market, ready to buy as much candy as they could.

And then, she saw her little brother. He smiled when he saw Mya. He ran to her and gave her a hug.

"I got you something," Mya said.

She handed him the giant chocolate bar. His hands reached out slowly, grasping the candy bar as if it would evaporate. His eyes lifted from the bar to his sister.

He didn't thank her. He couldn't say anything. But Mya knew. She could see it in his face.

The Getaway

Missouri

One gunshot. Fired directly into the air. That's all it took.

Ray's hand shook as he stood in the middle of the bank. The revolver, still smoking, pointed toward the ceiling. Time seemed to freeze; he had never shot a gun before.

He didn't know why he paused. It's not like he shot at a person. It was just a warning shot. But somehow, the noise made the robbery real.

He watched as grown men in three-piece suits sprawled across the floor, scampering behind table legs, pressing themselves against walls.

A gray fedora rocked upside down at Ray's feet. He noticed the red feather. And then he noticed the silence. Palpable.

"Come on!" James shouted. "Grab the cash from that register!"

Ray shook himself free from his daze and ran frantically to the register on the left. He pointed the gun at the bank teller, who shook with fear behind iron bars.

"Throw the cash in the bag!" Ray shouted. He shoved the bag through the bars. The teller took the bag and began to fill it slowly with bills. Ray looped one finger around his suspender, a nervous habit.

The teller was taking too long. He was only on the second cash register.

Whipping his head around in paranoia, Ray saw James following the banker toward the vault.

Returning his attention to the teller, Ray yelled, hoping to instill haste. The teller complied, but still seemed to dawdle.

"Thirty seconds!" James shouted from the vault.

They had it timed. Two minutes. In and out.

Ray banged his hand against the counter.

"Hurry up!" he shouted to the teller.

The bank's blinds were open, and Ray felt too much motion outside.

"That's fine," he yelled at the teller. "Just give me the bag. Toss it over"

The teller threw the bag over the iron bars. Ray allowed it to land on the floor before he lifted it and tied it off. He waved his revolver at James, who stood impatiently near the vault as the banker filled another pillowcase with cash.

"Let's go!" Ray shouted. "It's time!"

James sprayed a few bullets toward the ceiling, just enough to quell any thoughts of insurrection before the bandits made their getaway. As James grasped three cash bags in one fist, Ray noticed the gray fedora again. Kneeling, he picked it up and placed it on his head. Perfect fit, he thought. He ran his hand along the red feather to smooth it out.

James reached a half-sprint as he neared Ray, and they both ran toward the front door. Early morning sun beamed through the glass, accented by bronzed fixtures. Ray noticed the dust particles that hung in the air. And then he noticed the cops.

Three police vehicles were stationed along the curb. Seven

policemen stood behind their vehicles, guns drawn.

"Come out with your hands up," the chief bellowed. "It's over for you. We have the entire street locked down."

"What do we do?" Ray asked.

"We kick the doors open," James said. "Come out, guns blazing."

Ray's eyes widened. He allowed a laugh to slip from his mouth.

"We don't have a chance against 'em, Jimmy," Ray said. "You know what they did to the Culver twins at City Bank last month."

Ray knew he couldn't die. Well, he could. But he couldn't. He needed to make it out of the bank alive. And with the money. If he wanted his son to live, anyway.

The medical bills had started appearing. Slowly at first. Ray's job at the factory only afforded him so much until he had to make choices. Water or medical bills. Dinner or medical bills.

He thought he had paid enough to keep the insurance companies off his back for a little while. But the bills and notices seemed to flood his mailbox faster with each passing month.

Ray's neighbor, James, ran with a seedy crowd. And when Ray had asked his neighbor for help, he didn't hesitate to help. In fact, he planned the whole operation. A one-and-done.

Ray dropped his eyes. Two minutes, he thought. Should have cut it by thirty seconds.

Peering over his shoulder, Ray noticed a side door to the bank, nestled in an alcove near the south end of the counter.

"Follow me," Ray said.

James raised an eyebrow at Ray's assertiveness. Without watching to see if James followed, Ray dashed for the door.

This side of the bank didn't have windows, no blinds to lift, but no way for the cops to peer in, either.

"What if they're out there waiting for us?" James asked.

"You got a better idea?" Ray said.

James shrugged and gripped his money bags tightly. Reaching for the doorknob, Ray retracted his arm. He placed his gun in the shoulder holster beneath his coat.

"What are you doing?" James asked.

Ray returned the question with a smile before turning the doorknob.

Sun peered through the open space. Ray snuck a glance outside. Expecting to see another row of cop cars, he moved his head out of the door slowly. Finally, he forced his entire body outside.

Nothing.

Not a cop in sight. No pedestrians strolling. No cars honking. Just a brick building and a fire escape. The side door led to an alleyway, likely an entrance for armored cars that made weekly exchanges.

Flinging the door open, he waved to James. Both men dashed away from the bank, away from the cops. Gravel crunched under their feet as they sprinted through the alleyway.

"Our getaway car is out front," James said. "What do we do? The cops have the whole street surrounded."

"You're right," Ray said. "They'll catch us if we keep running. They'll have units searching the whole city for us."

They weaved between corridors until they ran out of concealed alleyways to follow. Opening their pathway onto an open street, James turned to Ray and smiled.

"Look at that old black roadster across the street," James said. "I'll bet that belongs to some bank owner. No way either of us will ever be able to afford one of those."

He winked and dashed across the street. Popping the door open, he slid into the driver's seat and fiddled with some wires. The engine revved. James waved to Ray, who sprinted across the street with his money bags. Tossing the bags in the trunk, Ray sat in the passenger seat. His nerves fired as the engine revved again.

"Where to, sir?" James mocked.

Ray smiled and shook his head. The car rolled away from the curb and cruised slowly down the street, turning left at the intersection.

"What are you doing?" Ray asked.

"Let's see how things are going," James said.

As the roadster sped down the street, Ray watched more cop cars flood the entrance to the bank.

Ray looked out the window in fear. But his worries were unfounded. All of the cops focused their attention on the bank's entrance.

James revved the engine a bit as he passed. One cop turned to look at the roadster. James returned the glance with a wink. The officer's face was dumbstruck.

The roadster weaved through the narrow city streets, until, finally, it pulled out of downtown. Stomping on the gas pedal, James pushed the roadster onto the interstate. Fast wind fluttered the red feather in Ray's fedora. Free.

The Fish

Montana

The water felt cold against Carson's foot, even through his waders. He took a second step into the shallow water, bracing himself for a change in force and balance. He gripped his fly rod with one hand and stripped some line from the reel. After generating some line momentum, he cast his fly upstream.

"Nice cast, Carson," Henry said.

Carson smirked.

"Not that I'm surprised," Henry continued. "You are my son, after all."

Henry stood downstream from his son, preparing to cast his own line into the river. He hadn't been fishing in the fall in a while. He felt rusty when it came to selecting which flies to use during this season.

"You know, when I was in my mid-twenties like you," Henry said, "I could pick a guaranteed fly with my eyes closed."

He smiled, reflecting back to earlier times.

"As you get older," Henry continued, "some things get more difficult. It gets tougher to find the time to do the things you love to do."

Carson didn't respond. He could have, but he didn't need to.

He recognized this as his father's own style of thinking through things. And Carson appreciated the imparted wisdom.

Henry cast his fly upstream, just below where Carson's fly had drifted. Carson recast his line upstream, this time, targeting a current closer to the river's edge where the fish would have more hiding places.

"Why do you love fishing so much, Dad?" Carson asked.

A lure to draw out some more wisdom from unexamined experiences.

"Oh, I don't know," Henry said. "I guess I just enjoy being outside."

Carson nodded while he tracked his fly drifting along the current. Henry's line had drifted toward fast-moving water, so he recast his line upstream.

"It's hard to get outside anymore," Henry continued. "For so many years, I spent so much time and energy in the office, looking at screens and papers and gray walls. It just got tough to get out of that rut."

A slight breeze kicked up, sending a few orange leaves onto the river. They floated and drifted for a while, but, eventually, they became soaked and began to sink. The breeze died immediately. Carson took four steps upstream and then recast, focusing on a current that backtracked, a quaint spot for fish to relax.

"But when I'm out here," Henry continued, "I feel free. I feel connected. Fishing is so simple. You have a moving river, swimming fish, amazing views, and silence. It gives you time to think. It's hard to find time to *really* think these days."

Carson nodded as he recast his line into the same target current.

"I definitely get that," Carson said. "I feel like I haven't had an original thought since elementary school. Everything is so shareable now; it's impossible to get away from all the noise."

"Yeah, you young ones have it tough," Henry said. "When I was your age, I used to come out to the river and just cast for hours. Just me. Up and down the river. The same cast. A singular focus."

Henry recast his line upstream. As soon as Henry's fly landed, Carson cast his own line upstream. His fly landed where the fast-moving current edged the slow-moving water.

"And, somehow, through that intensely focused mindset," Henry said, "I was really able to think."

Henry allowed the idea to continue to flow through his mind, swirling a little before transitioning into a related, yet altogether new thought.

"It's important to carve out that space for yourself, wherever it ends up being," Henry said. "Every person needs some space to let things ruminate. That's how we achieve true wisdom. We take the things we learn and our experiences, and we spend time letting those things swim around in our minds. And we need space to let that process happen."

An expression of clarity appeared on Henry's face. His line drifted, tightening the line. The fly bounced on top of the river.

Carson smiled at his father's moment of self-realization. Taking four more steps upstream, Carson cast his line into a deep pocket of slow-moving water.

Suddenly, his line tightened and began to run. Unsure if he had snagged a rock or hooked a fish, Carson set the hook. The line swirled around the pool.

"Dad!" Carson shouted. "Got one!"

Henry reeled his line in and walked over to Carson, who had

his net in the water. The end of his fly rod bowed.

As the fish settled in the net, Carson removed the hook and pulled the net just out of the water.

"Beautiful trout," Henry said. "You caught a good one today, son."

The Horizon

Nebraska

The school bell rang and the hallways filled with chatter and footsteps. High school students funneled from their classes to their lockers. Backpacks flung over shoulders, weighing down students with books and papers and expectations.

Reed bounced off of a football player's shoulder. He stumbled, but gained his composure and balance.

"Excuse me," Reed said.

He looked at the football player for a hint of reciprocal apology, but he had already moved down the hallway.

Typical, Reed thought.

Twisting his combination lock, Reed popped his locker open and grabbed his math book, along with a copy of a classic novel he needed to read for English class.

As he walked down the crowded hallway, he saw Emily standing with her boyfriend, Kevin. Reed didn't understand what she saw in Kevin. Aside from an accurate jump shot, he had the personality of lukewarm water and brains like mashed potatoes.

"I'll pick you up at seven," Kevin said. "I just got my truck washed, so it'll be nice and clean for you."

Emily smiled, a veneer, pretending like she cared about his oversized gas machine.

"What should we wear?" Emily asked.

Reed rolled his eyes, a gesture that no one else noticed. A benefit of being invisible. One day, Reed knew that Emily would see Kevin for who he really was. Or, who he really *wasn't*.

And then, she would see Reed in a different light.

But that wasn't happening in high school. Maybe it would happen after high school, after they all went their separate ways, after people stopped concerning themselves with juvenile popularity schemes.

He continued his walk through the hallway. As he walked, he felt himself floating, invisible to those in the upper levels of the high school social ladder. He weaved between letterman jackets and name brand shirts and people who made visible statements about their identities.

He knew that happened after high school too.

As Reed pushed the door open, he felt the chill of Nebraska's incoming winter. Winds blew cold air from somewhere far away. The fields carried a smell of impending dormancy.

"Reed," a sophomore said. "You going to the party tonight?"

"Can't make it tonight," Reed said. "I've got a family thing."

"So do I," the sophomore said.

Reed nodded, sharing an unspoken understanding that neither of them had a family event. They just didn't get invited to the party.

The rusted two-door car sat at the far end of the parking lot. Reed fished in his backpack for the keys. He grabbed them and unlocked his door. The old leather seats, insulated from the cold, had baked in the sun all day. They were faded, cracked

121

from decades of use and exposure to the elements. Reed was the newest owner of the car, an heirloom that had circulated through the family's youngest drivers for the last thirty years. He turned the key. The engine struggled to start, but it always did. Finally, the engine revved. Reed pressed the gas pedal and eased up on the clutch, smoothly rolling out of his parking spot.

The parking lot had thinned in a matter of minutes, but students lingered, talking about their days and their plans, unaware of their surroundings. Reed waited and weaved before he arrived at the parking lot exit.

As he pulled out, he rolled his driver side window down. The smell of chilled air breathed freshness into his stuffy car. The rough cement road bounced his car up and down, but the bounce soon became a rhythm. Guitar whined from the country song that came from his radio. The speakers crackled. The radio signal was fuzzy. It always was.

Reed turned west onto the two-lane highway. His family's house was a good ten miles from the school. The drive took him almost fifteen minutes. But he didn't mind it most days. It gave him time to think, to unwind from the stresses of the day. The math tests. The essays. The cafeteria table politics.

"This table's for basketball players only," one guy had said.

Reed put his head down and moved to another table full of misfits, brought together by their own isolation, but still isolated.

Sometimes, Reed wished he was home instead of at school. He didn't mind his house. And he didn't mind his family. They got along alright. His older brother had gone off to college last year. His younger sister was beginning to require more attention. Sometimes, Reed felt like he was just existing.

His car sped along the highway, passing a few cars moving in the opposite direction. The landscape around the road was flat in all directions. If he didn't already know where he was going, he'd be lost.

Sometimes, he felt like continuing his drive on the highway, just to see how far it went. Keep going west.

He could keep driving, straight into the horizon. Straight into the unknown, to a place where he could find himself in the uncharted lands of somewhere else. Somewhere that people appreciated each other's differences and nuances, their perspectives and identities. A place that celebrated something besides the flat landscape expanding in all directions.

Maybe he'd end up in California on the beach. Maybe he'd end up in the Rockies somewhere, snowboarding to school instead of driving down a dusty road. Or maybe in Portland with all the other weirdos he'd heard newscasters critiquing on the channel his mom always watched.

He wanted to be a weirdo. He *was* a weirdo. But there wasn't room for that in his town.

At least not yet.

The Gamble

Nevada

He was down seven hundred.

Ben lifted two chips from his dwindling pile and placed them in the circle. One hundred dollars. A standard bet. The dealer waved his hand from one side of the table to the other. All bets were final.

The dealer flipped a card and dropped it in front of Ben. A queen.

Good start, Ben thought. He didn't dare say it out loud.

The dealer placed a card in front of the other two players, and then one in front of herself. A six.

"Right where we want her," a player said.

Ben nodded, but felt hesitant about the player's preemptive declaration of victory. There was a lot of blackjack left to play. And the player had placed bad luck in the air.

The dealer flipped Ben's second card. He hoped for another face card to give him an even twenty. Maybe even an ace to give him twenty one. And an instant win.

"A five?" Ben said.

"Hey, at least she's showing a six," another player said.

The dealer flipped over her last card, laying it face down so no one at the table could see it. She looked at Ben. It was time for him to indicate his next move.

With a queen and a five, Ben had a fifteen. The dealer showed a six. He always had to assume that the dealer's hidden card was a ten. If she had a sixteen, she would have to hit, and the chances of her getting a face card was high. If she got a high card, she would go over twenty one and bust. Ben wins.

His only goal: beat the dealer.

He did not want another card to add to his fifteen. With his luck, he'd get a ten and push himself way over twenty one, forcing a bust. A loss.

"Stay," Ben said, waving his hand over the table.

The dealer nodded and moved to the next player. He waved his hand, indicating that he would stay. Another player did the same.

The dealer grabbed her six card and flipped over the hidden card.

"Come on, jack," a player said.

The dealer's hidden card flipped face up on the green felt.

A five.

Of course, Ben thought.

The dealer had to hit. She took a card from the deck and dropped it on the table.

"King," she said. "Twenty one."

The dealer grabbed all the chips and cards from their places on the green felt. Ben felt his hope drain away as the dealer took his hundred-dollar chips away. Now, Ben was down eight hundred.

The dealer removed the remaining cards from the deck and combined them with the discard pile. She shuffled and shuffled and shuffled, a process that gave Ben time to plan his next move.

And he needed a plan. Badly.

Ben's student loan debt weighed on his financial situation. For the last ten years, he hadn't saved anything. Not because he didn't want to. Not because he spent his money on frivolous things. Older folks always told him that, if the younger generation would stop buying coffee, they could all afford houses. A laughable piece of advice coming from someone who bought a house back then for the price of ten coffees today.

No. he hadn't saved any money because he couldn't. His monthly student loan payment was eating away at any extra income he had. And he still had ten years of payments to look forward to. At least.

When Ben went to college, he thought he was doing everything right. Get a government-approved loan, graduate with honors, get a job after college and pay off the loan quickly.

But the loan's high interest rate consumed any progress of paying the loan off. Even with a job as a data analyst, Ben's monthly salary barely kept him afloat after he paid his required loan minimum.

Ben had gone to a casino for the weekend to have some fun, to get away from the dullery of his desk job, the rut of student debt payments and bills and routine. He had a budget: one hundred dollars to spend on gambling. On his first blackjack hand, he bet a modest five dollars. The dealer gave him a jack and an ace, a clean twenty one. An easy win. The dealer passed a five dollar chip his way. He was up five bucks.

Things had gone bad quickly. And here he sat, eight hundred dollars down. Student debt looming, bills unpaid, his room charge hanging in the air. He was agonizing over the fact that he allowed himself to take it this far, that he had allowed himself to dive deeper into debt.

But the lingering thought of one big win kept him at the table.

So, he put another hundred dollars worth of chips on the green felt. Two green chips. The dealer waved her hand across the table.

"All bets are final," she said.

Ben knew the drill.

The dealer set a card down in front of Ben. A six. Ben dropped his head. He knew that he was in for another hundred dollar loss. The dealer gave cards to the other players before dropping a four in front of her. When she got back to Ben, she dropped another six in front of him.

Ben raised an eyebrow.

"Split," Ben said.

He knew it was a risky move, but he needed something big. He put another hundred dollars down on the table and the dealer split the sixes into two separate hands. She dealt a five to one hand and a four to another. Ben was looking at an eleven and a ten.

His eyebrow remained raised.

He had another risky move in his bag. He placed two stacks of chips at the top of both hands.

"Double down on both," Ben said.

The player next to him patted Ben on the back.

"There we go!" he shouted.

Ben knew it was a bold move. He would only receive one card for each hand from the dealer. He had four hundred dollars out on the table. If he lost both hands to the dealer, he would move into four-digit debt. A full month of student loan payments.

The dealer pointed to the six and five.

"Face down?" the dealer asked.

Ben craved the suspense.

"Sure," Ben said.

The dealer put a single card face down by the pile of eleven, and another single card face down by the pile of ten. He needed each pile to beat the dealer. Ideally, each pile would total twenty one and he wouldn't have to worry.

But, when the dealer flipped over her hidden card and showed a five, and then hit a king for a total of nineteen, Ben knew he was in trouble.

The dealer automatically stayed. And then, she reached for Ben's first hidden card. He needed a nine to beat the dealer. A ten to make twenty one.

"A queen!" the dealer said. "That's twenty one."

Ben clutched his chest in relief. But his relief escaped as the dealer reached toward the pile of ten. He needed another ten to beat the dealer, or an ace to seal a twenty one.

"An ace!" the dealer shouted.

Ben's hand found his chest again. He had won both hands. The dealer shoved four stacks of chips to Ben. Four hundred dollars. Ben's heart raced as he snatched the chips and placed them in his pile. He was beginning his climb out of the hole. He needed to win another four hundred to break even, and then keep going.

He felt bold. He felt alive. He put two hundred dollars in chips on the green felt. The dealer waved her hand, and then dealt Ben and ace. On her second pass, she placed a card down in front of Ben. He saw the ornate outline of someone royal. The entire table cheered.

The Drive

New Hampshire

Byron had always wanted to see the leaves. The rich oranges and reds on the broad maples that lined the narrow highways. The neverending pavement, painted with natural hues that shined with a fresh coat of rain, a river of ancient concrete through primeval forests.

He had talked about driving through the highways of New Hampshire when he retired. When he had more time. His wife in the passenger seat. Oldies playing from their stereo. The windows down. The smell of nature flowing through the car, paired with pleasant chatter and contemplative silence.

When he retired. When he had more time.

But today, it was Betty behind the wheel, guiding the old two-door car through the pristine wilderness of the Northeast. The early morning October sun flickered through the orange leaves, casting a golden hue into the air. Her window was cracked just enough to invite the crisp morning to linger in the car.

Oldies fluttered from the speakers. A familiar tune, a love song accented by calm piano. The singer's voice crackled through the old microphone from somewhere deep in history.

129

Somewhere deep in Betty's memory.

"I love this song," Betty said. "And it's such a beautiful morning."

She looked over to the passenger seat and smiled. The edges of her eyes crinkled, revealing worn wrinkles from years of laughter.

Her marriage was special.

Betty's memories drifted, landing on the moment she met Byron. He was a junior in college down in Boston. She was a sophomore. They both studied English. Not that she knew it then. Betty had been sitting on a bench reading when Byron walked by, his head down, powering toward something important. And then, he tripped. His books flew across the lawn. He laid still for a moment, catching his breath and his composure. As he sat up, his eyes connected with Betty.

They dated through college and, after that, decided to get married and have children. Byron's job bounced the family around the East Coast for a while.

"We should go check out the leaves this autumn," Betty said. "The kids would love it. And it's something you've always talked about doing."

"I just can't believe that I've lived on the East Coast my whole life and I've never seen the New Hampshire leaves in the fall," Byron said.

Betty smiled. She knew that her husband felt the weight of routine on his mind. But she also knew that he needed time to decompress.

"Let's go next weekend," Betty said.

Byron rubbed his neck, shackled by his own schedule.

"Too busy this fall, dear," Byron said. "Maybe next year."

Next year came and went. The kids transformed into adults

with their own lives, their own schedules. As they moved out, Betty thought it would be the ideal time to venture to New Hampshire and look at the leaves.

"For the first autumn in years, the kids aren't playing sports," Betty said. "Let's drive up north and see the leaves."

Byron rubbed his neck. He wanted to see the leaves. They brought so much peace, so much freedom, even in the face of change. And the idea of carelessly coasting through the forest, no worries or obligations, just Byron and Betty and the scenery, that was an idea that appealed to him.

But he just needed to wait a few more years. He needed to wait until life slowed down.

"We don't have a free weekend this fall," Byron said. "But I've only got a few years until retirement. Then, we'll have all the time in the world."

Then cancer hit Byron.

Within a few months, he was gone. And Betty was alone.

Understandably, Betty grieved. She sulked and sat in her house, afraid to go out because going out would mean answering questions. It would mean facing well-intentioned people who constantly reminded her of her husband's death with phrases like "I'm so sorry about Byron."

One Thursday morning, Betty looked outside and saw that the green leaves on a tree in her backyard had turned a soft yellow. She grabbed her car keys. And she drove north.

She played Byron's favorite songs from the stereo as she wove through cities and towns on the way to the untamed forest.

Her old car hummed along the concrete before it provided a path to peace. She watched the unique reds and oranges and yellows and greens fuse together, blending into something that Betty could only describe as nature.

Some leaves remained green. New and full of life, so much potential before them. Others, red with age, looked ready to drop, ready to contribute to the forest floor.

Then, as Betty looked out the window, she saw a single leaf fall from a tree. It landed on her windshield. The leaf's veins, worn from its struggle for life, provided a beautiful canvas of color. Vibrant orange.

She smiled, her eyes crinkling on the edges. Betty looked over to her empty passenger seat.

"All the time in the world," Betty said.

The Trash

Ella gripped the handle and planted her foot on the grated metal step. The garbage truck revved its engine and sent vibrations across the entire vehicle. Ella jolted as it accelerated. She tightened her grip.

The truck moved slowly along the street to the next house. There was a lot of space between houses in this neighborhood. Ella watched the metal posts in the ornate, iron fences as the truck sped by. The posts seemed to blur together, nearly sending Ella into a hypnotic trance.

But then the truck stopped. Ella was up.

She sprang from the step and ran to the garbage can. She gripped it with both hands, her gloves providing the necessary grip to hoist the garbage can to her partner. Together, they flipped the can's contents into the truck's massive trash compartment. Ella grabbed the empty garbage can and returned it to its proper place by the curb.

"Look at that," Ella said. "All those broken down boxes of new stuff."

Her partner, Simon, shook his head.

"Rich folks," he said. "Always getting new stuff to replace

133

their older new stuff."

Ella grabbed the handle and braced herself for the truck's acceleration. As the truck moved toward the next house, Ella peered into the trash compactor. She saw it all. A television that looked unused, followed by a box for a larger television. A vacuum that looked functional sitting atop the box for a robotic vacuum. Half-eaten plates of food. Dozens of coffee cups from trendy coffee shops. Plastic wrap from unseen boxes. Plastic peanuts to protect the contents of whatever was in those boxes. Plastic bottles, still half-filled with soda.

"I can't believe people still drink soda," Ella shouted over the engine's roar.

"Why not?" Simon asked.

"Do you know what soda is made of?" Ella asked.

"Nope," Simon said.

"Exactly," Ella said.

The truck stopped and Ella jumped off. She grabbed the trash can by the handles and handed one side to Simon. They tipped the can over and watched its contents fall into the truck. Ella sprinted back to the curb, dropped the can off, and returned to her post on the truck.

"Did you see that?" Simon asked.

"See what?" Ella said.

"That whole turkey," Simon said. "And a barely-eaten fruit tray. And a bottle of something that I've only heard about in rap songs."

Ella raised an eyebrow.

"These people are throwing away some serious money on food they didn't even eat," Simon said.

Ella shook her head. She hated to see good food go to waste. The truck stopped, Ella and Simon dumped the trash, and the truck moved again. The routine was familiar, safe. Ella had been on this same truck with Simon for the last seven years. Sure, the days were monotonous, but the pay was steady. And, if she worked long enough, she would have a pension for retirement. Only 23 more years.

Ella enjoyed looking at the houses in this neighborhood. This was an old money block. The houses were mostly brick. Old iron gates around them, covered in vines. Long driveways with expensive cars. Pitched roofs. Ornate windows. A few houses even had those castle-looking towers. It was childish, but Ella always imagined that archers waited up there, ready to shoot down invaders who stormed the gates.

Sometimes, Ella imagined herself storming the gates.

The truck sped out of the neighborhood and crossed the highway. The houses grew smaller, more compact. Eventually, the small houses seemed to stack on top of each other before turning into apartments and dense tenements. Elegant iron gates were transformed into chain link fences.

Ella jumped off the truck as it pulled into the garage. She waved to the driver and to Simon. She took off her gloves and stuck them into her jacket pocket. She unzipped the top of her coveralls and let it dangle around her waist. Her boots thumped against the concrete as she rounded the corner to her apartment.

"Hey, Ella!" a familiar voice shouted from across the street.

"Good morning, Mrs. Gracie," Ella shouted back. "How's that grandson of yours doing?"

"Oh, he's the sweetest little man," Mrs. Gracie said.

"He takes after you," Ella shouted. "Have a good day, now."

Mrs. Gracie waved to Ella, who returned the wave with a kind smile.

Ella loved her neighborhood. It wasn't as glamorous as the old money houses, but it was more comfortable. People actually waved to each other because they always came into contact. No one hid behind money and iron gates around here.

Unlocking the door to her apartment, Ella stomped up the stairs. Most of the doors in the hallway were open. She heard a mom yell to her kids that breakfast was ready. She heard the sounds of a record player coming from another room. The smell of bacon floated through the hallway. Finally, she reached her apartment door.

Her apartment was silent. Looking into the living room, she noticed her television: small and old. She took off her boots, washed her hands, and opened the refrigerator. It was nearly empty, aside from some milk. She reached into the cupboard and grabbed the pancake mix.

The sound of small footsteps muffled into the kitchen.

"Mommy," the little girl said, "how was riding the big truck?"

Ella smiled.

"It was eye-opening, as always, my girl," Ella said.

She picked up her daughter, who clung to Ella's neck.

"Good," the girl said. "Are you making pancakes for us?"

"I sure am, baby girl," Ella said. "It's not much."

The little girl smiled and gave her mom a kiss on the cheek.

"Anything you make for me is the best," the girl said. "I love you, Mommy."

Ella smiled and stirred the pancake batter.

"I love you, too."

The Balloon

Fire erupted from the burners, sending a six-foot flame cascading toward the sky. Heat scalded the crisp air. Michael's knuckles crunched beneath the hot metal, beneath his gloves, beneath the ropes and levers. As he looked across the field, he saw hundreds of flames.

"More and more every year," Michael shouted above the roar of the flame.

His daughter, Kelly, looked at him intently as she deciphered his inaudible message.

"There sure are," Kelly shouted back.

Michael nodded, and then reduced the flame before closing off the gas completely.

"Looks like that's ready to roll," Kelly said.

"And now, we wait," Michael said.

The winds looked favorable. Low wind speed, blowing slightly east. They had a few minutes before they needed to fill their balloon with heat.

Kelly looked out of the wicker basket and saw their balloon sprawled across the grass. It looked so weak when it wasn't full. Wrinkly, like an old trash bag. But she saw its power. Its

137

potential.

As her eyes drifted upward toward the field, she saw a balloon begin to fill with warmth. It slowly lifted off the grass.

"Dad," Kelly said, "that red one is starting. Should we?"

Michael was leaning against the wicker basket. He turned his head and watched the balloon.

"They went a little too soon," Michael said. "This is one of those instances when I want to be a part of the group."

"But then no one will notice our balloon," Kelly said.

Michael smiled.

"That's the point," he said.

Kelly gave her dad a look that she had given him a thousand times. A look that expressed confusion, rebellion, and obedience.

A neon blue balloon began to fill up near the middle of the field.

"Now it's time," Michael said.

Kelly rolled her eyes and jumped out of the wicker basket onto the grass. She grabbed a rope and began to maneuver the deflated balloon. Michael aimed the burner toward the opening in the balloon canvas. And he fired. Little bursts at first, just enough to get some heat into the balloon's narrow opening. Between bursts, he heard echoes of flames throughout the entire field. Everyone was getting ready. Not on command from some all-powerful general, but synchronized with the collective mind.

As the balloon filled, it began to rise. The sun rose behind it, sending beams of colorful light dancing into the field. The balloon's vibrant purple and teal canvas continued to grow. Michael always loved this part, seeing the balloon transform from something useless to something so massive, so powerful.

Finally, the balloon was ready. It hovered above the wicker basket, poised for takeoff. Kelly jumped into the basket with her dad. She looked across the field and saw hundreds of balloons inflating, waiting, hovering.

And then, with seemingly no instructions, one balloon lifted from the field, pulling its wicker basket with it.

Another balloon followed.

"Here we go," Michael said. "You ready?"

"Can't wait," Kelly said.

Michael reached for the level that controlled the flame, but he paused. His hand hovered.

"You want to take us up?" Michael asked.

Kelly smiled. She had always wanted to send the first flame into the balloon. Her dad had offered before, but Kelly felt too hesitant, too inexperienced.

But this time was different.

"Can I really?" Kelly asked.

Michael stepped to the side and made room for Kelly. She reached for the lever, sending a powerful shower of flames into the balloon's opening. The heat from the flame startled her, and the force from the gas jolted her knees. But she held strong.

After a few bursts of flame, Kelly evened out the pressure. She felt butterflies in her stomach as the wicker basket lifted off the ground.

"You did it!" Michael shouted over the roar of the flame.

Kelly hugged her dad, and then made room for him to regain control of the balloon.

Kelly looked at the engine. It had always scared her slightly, the fact that an open flame was so close to a wicker basket. But the idea of rising so calmly, that had always brought her peace.

The balloon rose higher and higher. Kelly was busy double-checking her dad's maneuvers and lever control and the gas tank gauges. Finally, the balloon reached a cruising altitude.

"Take a look at that view," Michael said.

Kelly was used to amazing aerial views. She had ridden in the balloon with her dad plenty of times. But, as she approached the edge of the wicker basket, she knew that this view was something different.

The mountains rose somewhere in the distance, illuminated by the golden hue of morning. But she wasn't focused on the mountains.

Hundreds of balloons filled the air around her, above her, beneath her. Reds, oranges, blues. Geometric patterns and clever designs. Hot air balloons from all over the West, floating in unison, propelled by the wind. Close together, but far enough apart. One collective mind working toward the same goal: wonder.

Kelly knew what this scene looked like from the ground. She had seen the pictures. But being a part of the beauty was something different altogether.

Lost in the view, Kelly barely noticed the balloon's descent. The other balloons descended too. A calm drop in altitude. A peaceful return to the ground.

When Michael's balloon landed, Kelly helped him drape the balloon onto the grass. The clean-up process was extensive.

"Let's get going," Michael said.

Kelly sat on the wicker basket. She watched as hundreds of balloon pilots packed up their aircrafts. Hundreds of individuals continued to work toward that common end. Everyone doing their part to provide a little more beauty for the world to see. Everyone taking time out of their day to make the world seem just a little bit brighter, if only for a moment.

"What are you waiting for?" Michael asked.

Kelly smiled. She jumped off the wicker basket and grabbed a rope from her dad and started pulling the balloon canvas. Michael stepped back and smiled before grabbing another rope to do his part.

The Money

Braxton stood alone in the elevator. He looked down and saw his own reflection in his shoes. His eyes drifted upward toward the reflective door. He noticed his own suit, still pressed after a long day at the office. A long day of trading, of analyzing spreadsheets and algorithms, of making calls and making deals. And, through all that, his suit still looked new.

It better, Braxton thought. *I paid enough for it.*

He smiled at his reflection in the elevator, but caught himself before the door opened, returning his face to its usual position, somewhere between a glare and a smirk. He walked through the lobby, his footsteps charged with purpose.

His pace hadn't always been so linear. When he arrived at the firm ten years ago, he stared at the lobby's gaudy chandeliers, its ornate decor, and its lofted ceilings that sent back an echo of each footstep. But these days, Braxton had too much on his plate. Too much money to worry about.

The sliding door opened and Braxton walked into the city, greeted by millions of honking cars and the scent of the sewer and the reflection of the setting sun off of glass-plated skyscrapers.

"Excuse me, sir," an old woman said. She sat on the concrete against the exterior wall of the building.

"What?" Braxton said, still walking.

"Could you spare some change for a hungry old woman?" she said.

Braxton raised an eyebrow and spit air. He quickened his step as if the sidewalk around her would contaminate his shoes. And he had just gotten them shined.

"Get a real job," Braxton muttered.

He stepped away from the woman and continued his walk. His shoes slapped the concrete in quick, disjointed steps. Braxton had places to be.

Well, one place. Happy hour.

Some of the other brokers got together every Thursday after work to grab a drink at a swanky bar. Braxton rarely went. He rarely left the office. But today, he needed to swing a deal with someone that a broker knew.

As he approached the entrance to the bar, he saw another person sitting against an exterior wall. An old man. He held out a small cup.

"Anything helps," the old man said.

Braxton looked down at his watch and pretended the man didn't exist. The door to the bar opened. Someone walked out. Braxton didn't have time for some old man who barely made time for his own situation. He needed to be in the bar. He needed to be in the room to make the deal happen. As the door began to close, he caught it and hustled into the bar, allowing the old man to dissipate from his memory.

* * *

Braxton's alarm woke him up much earlier than sunrise. He sat up in bed and clutched his temples. He had a headache. Not from drinking too much. He only had one drink, using it more as a prop than a social enhancer. The deal was made outside of the office, in a backroom bar, like most big deals.

It wasn't the gin and tonic. But what was it?

Something nagged at Braxton's mind.

He walked over to the window and saw himself in the reflection. His hair looked disheveled, much more than usual. But he didn't mind.

After a shower and shave, he put on a new suit, dark green with a black shirt beneath it. He placed a layer of cash in his money clip and put it in his back pocket. Tightening his tie and fastening his cufflinks, he looked in the mirror and forced himself to smile. Dressing up made him feel a little more normal. But something still dug into his brain. Walking to his kitchen, he opened the refrigerator. He felt a strange sensation of hunger without appetite, so he closed it and took the elevator to the lobby.

"Maybe a walk to work will help me clear my head," Braxton said.

The doorman nodded to Braxton as if the comment had been directed toward him.

The sun rose, sending beams of light through the narrow spaces between skyscrapers. Some reflected off of exterior windows and passing taxis. Each glare reminded Braxton that his mind was uneasy.

As he neared the front door of his office, he saw her. The same old woman without a home, without a job. The same old woman that begged him for spare change every single day.

I don't have time for this, Braxton thought.

He jogged across the street, slowing to a stroll when he landed on the sidewalk. The old woman sat in her usual spot. She looked like she lacked resources, basic necessities like reliable food and water and a roof most days.

Braxton felt a jolt of pain surge through his head. He stopped and grabbed his temples again. Through the pain, he felt embarrassed, or at least the threat of embarrassment. He didn't want to appear weak in front of his office. When he opened his eyes, he looked around to see if anyone had noticed. And no one seemed to care, passing him while looking down at their phones, or their own shoes.

Everyone except the old woman. She looked at Braxton with an expression of genuine concern. Of empathy. Of care.

"Are you alright, sir?" the old woman asked.

Suddenly, Braxton realized that he was alright. His headache had evaporated.

"Yes," Braxton said. "Yes, I'm fine."

The old woman nodded. Braxton returned the nod, a simple acknowledgment that the old woman existed. A simple gesture that he had failed to give her every single day. Until today.

Braxton looked at his watch, and then up the tower toward his office. And then, he returned his attention to the old woman.

"Excuse me, ma'am," Braxton said. "Have you eaten anything yet today?"

The old woman shook her head. Braxton could see the pride that she used to mask her embarrassment, to conceal the effect of the stigma.

"Would you like to go grab breakfast at the bagel shop on the corner?" Braxton asked.

The old woman smiled. She stood slowly from her sitting

position, stretching her legs and her joints, allowing her eyes to crinkle along with her smile, deep set wrinkles that she hadn't accessed in a long time.

She reached out her hand. And Braxton took it in his own.

"That would be lovely," she said.

The Restaurant

North Carolina

The fluorescent lights hummed as Miles flipped the switch. The familiar smell of last night's menu wafted toward him. He used to love the smell of barbecue, but now, it carried a certain weight to it. The kind of weight that can crush a hobby once it became a chore.

"Heyyo, Miles," the cook shouted from the kitchen.

"Good to see ya, Joe," Miles shouted.

Miles and Joe had greeted each other the same way for the last 25 years. Joe was a young kid, still in high school when Miles hired him. He'd watched as Joe grew up and started a family of his own. Miles had hired Joe right after he opened up his barbecue joint: *Miles and Q*.

It all started in the backyard. Before it was an official business. Miles would fire up his smoker and let ribs roast for hours. Sauce-smothered chicken wings sizzled to perfection. Bratwursts, slightly charred. He'd boil up baked beans, fire-grill corn cobs soaked in butter, and bake cornbread in his cast-iron skillet. And then, he'd invite the entire neighborhood.

Miles's family loved it. Always social. Always well-fed.

Naturally, people always said things like, "Miles, when are

you going to open up your own restaurant?" As if operating a successful restaurant came down to the simple idea of cooking good food.

Enough people praised Miles's barbecue that he finally decided to quit his job at the phone service and started his own restaurant. He set up his barbecue joint in a small, wooden shack just off the highway. Trees surrounded the back patio. There was enough space for two smokers and a small kitchen, enough room to cook up some side dishes.

The flow of people was slow at first. But through word-of-mouth, the gravel parking lot began to fill up, especially around dinnertime.

And not much had changed in 25 years. Miles's place had become a local favorite. He had regulars. He had the occasional out-of-towner who stumbled upon the random stretch of highway. Sometimes, foodies from big cities came by to check out the local cuisine. And they always brought their snooty attitudes with them. Mostly, Miles liked the regulars.

"I got that brisket smoking out back," Joe said. "What else do we want to go with tonight?"

Miles looked at the list of meat supplies that hung on the wall.

"Let's go with chicken thighs tonight," Miles said. "We still got a lot from our last shipment."

"You got it," Joe said.

Miles lingered by the supply list. Something was off with Miles's demeanor, and Joe noticed. Joe looked at Miles, waiting for a follow-up thought, an off-handed comment that might give him some insight into Miles's unusually downcast demeanor. But Miles gave him nothing. Instead, he walked into the back office and shut the door. Joe shrugged and returned his attention to the kitchen.

Miles loved barbecue. He loved making it. He loved eating it. He loved *sharing* it. But the daily grind of meat supply, customer interactions, accounting, and marketing had taken its toll on Miles. He felt stuck, chained to the same routine. No way out. No excitement. His senses felt dull.

"This meat is too crispy," customers said.

"My soda is too flat," customers said.

"There's not enough sauce on my ribs," customers said.

"It smells too smokey out here," customers said.

Then go somewhere else, Miles thought.

Miles felt a familiar pressure building in his mind. He took one final drink of his coffee and put his head down on the desk. He closed his eyes. Just for a minute.

* * *

When he awoke, the light in the room had shifted. It had taken on a distinct golden hue. He'd slept through his preparation window. His heart began to pound. Customers were here.

I'll bet Joe has it covered, Miles thought.

His heart rate slowed. He felt himself move back into the grind, into the rut, into the monotony of the same thing, day in and day out. Cooking for people who didn't really appreciate it.

Miles opened the door to his office and walked into the kitchen. Joe nodded as he stirred a massive pot of baked beans.

"You good, Miles?" Joe asked.

"Yeah, I'm fine," Miles said. "I just needed to shake the cobwebs off."

"Well, I hope you shook 'em," Joe said. "We've got a packed

house tonight."

Miles walked through the kitchen onto the patio. The scent of brisket smoke and family laughter filled the air. All nine picnic tables were full.

Miles leaned against the wall and watched. Mothers handed pieces of ribs to their sons. Fathers shared cornbread with daughters. Grandparents and grandchildren laughed through sauce-covered faces.

Pushing off the wall, Miles walked through the picnic tables. He noticed a couple who seemed out of place. Their clothes were a little too stiff. Their eyes were a little too wide. Their dialect was a little too precise.

"I can't believe we have to share a picnic table with someone else," the man whispered.

"It's a family-style kind of restaurant," the woman said. "Besides, it's just for one meal."

"It's unprofessional," the man said. "Not classy at all."

Miles forced himself to maintain a smile, but he felt his spirit dampen. Out-of-towners always seemed to complain about something.

"And this brisket," the man continued. "It's too charred. To dry."

An old woman from the other side of the table raised an eyebrow.

"I don't understand why people down here eat this junk anyway," the man continued.

The old woman whipped her head toward the couple.

"If y'all want to complain about it so much," she shouted, "go somewhere else then."

The man's face whitened. He shook with nervousness.

"You order burnt ends," the old woman said. "That's why they charred. Know your barbecue before you start complaining."

The man leaned forward, ready to engage in battle. The old woman was unphased.

"This here is a North Carolina treasure. The best barbecue you'll ever have in your life," the old woman continued. "If you're going to sit here and complain about it, we don't want you."

Miles smiled. His eyes lit up. The woman looked at Miles and winked.

"And this man behind you is the owner," the old woman said. "He cooks for this community seven days a week for the last 25 years. This community would be nothing without him. So you'd better turn around and thank him for your meal."

The man turned and faced Miles. His eyes projected obedience.

"Thank you for my meal, sir," the man said.

"You're quite welcome," Miles said. "I hope you enjoy it."

Miles turned around and continued his walk through the crowd. He heard laughter echo from table to table. Somewhere deep in his soul, he laughed too.

The Land

North Dakota

The land rolled over the horizon, vast and sparse with wild grass. A river cut through the rock formations that took millions of years to craft. Layers of compressed sediment, different hues of natural reds and browns, carved out to show us the land's story.

But most couldn't read it anymore.

Eve stood in front of her tent. The sky was clear and she could see her breath like smoke in front of her face. She burrowed into her jacket, wishing the water would boil faster so she could make tea.

"Ready?" Imani asked.

Eve looked at the hot water. It had just started boiling. She poured some hot water in her mug and turned off the burner.

"I sure am," Eve said.

Imani jumped into the driver's side of the Jeep. Eve took the passenger side. She put her tea mug in the cup holder and stashed her backpack beneath her feet. The Jeep's engine revved as Imani propelled it forward. It crawled over the mounds of dust and gravel along the dirt road, a pathway that wasn't traveled often.

"We should be there in a few minutes," Imani said. "Get your camera ready."

Eve reached into her backpack and removed her camera. She checked the lens and the settings to make sure that her camera was ready to capture what they found.

"I hope this trek gives us what we've been looking for," Imani said. "Otherwise, they might pull our funding."

"And all this would have been for nothing," Eve said.

The Jeep pulled into an open patch of dirt. Imani jumped out and opened the back door, grabbing her kit and a small shovel. She walked through the grass toward a rocky outcropping. Eve followed close behind, waiting with her finger on the camera's trigger. As they moved closer to the rock face, Eve noticed the defined lines of rock, different colors layered on top of others. A prehistoric canvas of nature.

"See the dark red line in the rock?" Imani asked. "It should be just below it."

They pushed their way through tall grass until they came to the rock face. Moving a large patch of grass to the side, Imani smiled.

"There it is!" she shouted. "They were right."

A small opening to a cave that led to a larger cavern within the layers of rock. Imani doubted that she could find the cave, but the Lakota woman that she spoke to had given perfect directions. It had taken Imani and Eve weeks to set up interviews and trek through the undefined line between borders and ancestral lands. But here they were. And here it was.

Imani pulled a flashlight from her backpack. She led the way into the cave's small opening. As Eve entered, she felt a dramatic drop in temperature, adding to the already cold morning. The dark crevasses and echoes sparked the fear that a bear would emerge at any moment.

But they pressed forward.

After a few twists and turns, they came to a large opening, deep under the earth that rose above them. Eve and Imani flashed their lights around on the ground, looking for the evidence. But they found little distinguishing features.

Until their flashlights moved upward.

A massive cave wall was illustrated with dozens of cave paintings. Some thousands of years old. Some maybe only centuries. Reds, blacks, and oranges depicted hunts, unions, and fears.

"We did it," Eve whispered.

Imani couldn't respond. But she didn't need to.

Eve pulled her camera close to her eye and snapped a picture of the entire wall, fitting it all into the frame. And then she stepped closer, framing an individual image from the wall: a human form dancing around a fire.

Imani removed a brush and a small trowel from her kit. She started digging beneath the paintings and etchings. Gradually, small fragments of tools, charcoal, and clothing appeared in the dirt. She dusted them with the brush, careful to preserve their integrity.

"Look at this," Imani said, pointing to a piece of charcoal. "This means that a group used this cave as shelter at some point."

Eve took a picture of the charcoal next to the brush.

"And this," Imani continued, motioning to a small piece of leather. "This might have come from an artist's coat, or shoe, or something."

Eve knelt down and snapped a picture of the embroidered

leather.

"We need more time, more people, and more evidence," Imani said, "but the fact that this is here means that we can keep researching."

Eve stood and smiled.

"And it means that the oil company can't destroy this place to line their own pockets by ripping up the earth," Eve said.

"We did it," Imani said.

They continued to excavate, taking pictures of their work to prove their case. Finally, as the cave warmed with the rising sun, they decided to leave. Jumping back in the Jeep, they knew that they would return. Maybe later that day. Maybe next week with a team. But they knew that they had preserved this place. And by preserving this place, they knew that a people could rest a little easier, could find some fragment of justice in a world that wanted to tear it apart, a world that couldn't remember how to read its own story.

The Front Lawn

Ohio

The man reached down and grabbed the crank, pulling it toward him with unnecessary force. The lawn mower's engine churned and churned before fully kicking on. A plume of exhaust smoke surged from the motor before dissipating into the formerly crisp air of the neighborhood.

"Works every time," the man said.

He pushed the lawn mower in a straight line toward the tree at the far end of his front yard. When he reached the edge of the grass, he dipped the handle and spun the mower before returning to the other end of the lawn. He focused his attention on the tire tracks from his last pass, rolling the wheels alongside them with precision.

The lines needed to be perfect. All the other neighbors had perfect lines.

A neighbor strolled down the sidewalk. Her dog strutted in front of her, connected to a thin leash. The dog was well-groomed and well-mannered. A red bandana sat around its neck.

"Hey, neighbor!" the dog owner shouted.

He cut the engine and stood next to his lawn mower, ready

to engage in conversation with one of his new neighbors.

"Good morning!" the man shouted. "Nice day for a walk."

"It sure is," the neighbor said.

She looked at the lawn. A smile began to appear on her face. But, as her eyes drifted toward the house, the smile faded before it formed. She clutched the dog leash and continued her stroll.

"Have a good one!" the man shouted.

He allowed his shoulders to drop for a moment before reinforcing his stoic demeanor. He reached down and yanked the lawn mower pulley and the engine revved back to life. Back to crafting his perfect lawn.

The man pushed his mower carefully along the wheel line. He put more effort and attention into this than he did at his regular job. Then again, his regular job didn't require much care. Or maybe he just didn't care about it enough to pay attention.

The lawn, on the other hand, required his attention. His house was modest, a mediocre, single-level house. Fine by most standards. But not in this neighborhood. Not on this street, where old houses had been revamped and restored to look worthy of a magazine cover.

The man knew that neighbors walked by and looked at his shabby house. His small shack. With every glance, the man felt his pride erode. With his job, he couldn't afford to move to a bigger house anytime soon.

But he could keep his lawn looking good.

He knew that people tended to judge a person based on their lawn. He did, anyway.

In practice, a lawn was pointless. It didn't yield any crops. It didn't provide space for any useful activities. But that was the point: pointlessness. The frivolous use of space showed everyone that he didn't need to use that space for growing food because he had throw-away money to spend on watering useless space. Green grass meant that someone had extra money to water their lawn excessively, even during the summer heat. Keeping it manicured showed that someone either had extra money to pay for that upkeep, or they had extra time because they had so much money. Either way, a green, manicured lawn displayed a certain level of status, the entryway into every homeowner's private castle.

It took the man a long time to mow his lawn, but he often wondered if his lawn could be bigger. He wondered if he needed a riding lawn mower. The bigger houses a few blocks down, some of them had riding lawn mowers.

A neighbor turned the corner, red-faced and winded from a slow, lumbering jog. He didn't want to talk to the man, but he did need a reason to stop and catch his breath.

"Lawn looks good," the neighbor said.

"Thanks," the man said. "It's tough to keep it up in this weather."

"Keep it up, and your lawn might look like the one across the street," the neighbor said.

The neighbor waved and continued his jog. The man wiped sweat from his forehead. He felt his own face redden, his own breath quicken.

As the lawn mower chugged along the grass, the man allowed his attention to drift toward the front lawns of other houses on the block. And the more he looked, the more he realized that they all looked the same. The houses. The cars. The lawns. All the same. Yet, somehow, he knew that if his lines were straighter, his house would stand out above the rest. He would receive the adoring attention of a casual jogger, a weekend dog walker, glaring with envy at his groomed grass.

The smell of gasoline and cut grass floated through the air, amplified with every pass of the lawn. Sweat continued to form on the man's forehead, eventually staining his gray shirt with dark spots. When the center of the grass was cut, he completed one full circle of the lawn to even out his rotation lines. And then he cut the engine and leaned against his mower.

"Looks good," the man whispered.

For now, anyway. One day, he thought, he would move to a bigger house in a better neighborhood. A neighborhood with a little more prestige, a little more notoriety.

And a bigger front lawn.

The Gift

Oklahoma

Mariana's backpack felt lighter than usual. The bulk bag of caramel apple lollipops had dwindled over the past months. Autumn. Prime season for selling the product.

"Your bus is gonna be here in five minutes!" Mom bellowed up the stairs.

Taking one last look in the mirror, Mariana checked her braids. Smooth and tight. She smiled and sauntered down the steps to the kitchen.

"Grab that toast and hustle out there, baby," Mom said.

Mariana snatched the toast off the counter. For a moment, she looked around the kitchen for Dad, but she already knew he was at work. Left before she woke up. Probably come home after she went to bed. Another double shift.

"Thanks, Mom," Mariana said.

She walked toward the door, but she stopped for a moment. Her eyes drifted to a frame on the wall with a picture of Mom. Mariana stepped closer to the picture. Black and white, a little grainy. Narrowing her eyes, Mariana focused on Mom's necklace. A thin silver chain with a silver heart. Mom was smiling in the photo, one of those genuine smiles that Mariana didn't see much anymore. Mom had been different since it happened.

"Bye, Mom!" Mariana shouted. "Love you."

She closed the door behind her and hopped down the stairs, passing a few apartments on the way. The door on the left never opened. Mariana thought an old lady lived there, but she wasn't sure. One of the apartments on the ground level, that's where Isaac lived. One time, she got to wave to him before he got in his mom's car and drove to school, so Mariana usually slowed down when she walked by his door.

But not today. She was late.

Mariana jogged to the corner of the block. The usual group waited in their usual spots. Jamaal leaned against the stop sign. He didn't talk much, probably thought he was too cool to talk to seventh graders. Hassan sat on the low brick wall, keeping his eyes down. Mariana understood. A sixth grader on a mostly upperclassmen bus would make any kid nervous. Dawn stood in the middle of the sidewalk, feet spaced evenly apart, glaring straight forward. But her eyes softened when she saw Mariana approach.

"Hey, Mar," Dawn said. "Thought you weren't coming today."

"I'm just running a little late," Mariana said.

Dawn raised an eyebrow. She had heard this before.

"You good?" Dawn asked.

"Yeah, I'm good," Mariana said. "I've just got a lot on my mind."

Dawn stepped toward Mariana, ready to ask for more details, but the bus churned around the corner, its brakes squawking as it stopped near the curb. Mariana climbed up the stairs and sat in her usual seat near the middle, just beyond the seat where the wheel stuck up and captured precious legroom.

The ride to school wasn't long. Mariana stared out the window. Dawn sat in the seat behind her, talking about her little brother and how annoying he was, but Mariana's thoughts continued to drift.

When she got to school, she walked to her locker. She spun the lock and perched her backpack on the shelf, open just enough to reach inside quickly and discreetly.

"What's good, Mariana?" a seventh grader said, leaning against the lockers.

"What you want?" Mariana asked.

"Lemme get two," he said.

Mariana stuck out her hand and the boy placed two dollar bills in her palm. Closing her grip, Mariana reached into her backpack and pulled out two caramel apple pops. The boy nodded and grabbed them, looking over his shoulder to make sure no teachers were watching. He put one in his pocket and unwrapped the other and merged into the crowded hallway.

Only five left, Mariana thought. *I can sell those by the end of the day*.

She needed to offload the last five lollipops before school ended. Actually, before lunch ended. So, during math class, she planned her sales approach. Five lollipops; five bucks. Overpriced, sure. But they were rare, and its price gave it status. Usually, customers came to her. Word of mouth told kids that Mariana sold by her locker before first period and after seventh.

But Mariana didn't want to wait until seventh period. She couldn't.

She needed to capitalize on the other best time for lollipop sales: lunch time in the cafeteria.

Stale pizza and charred something marinated through

the huge space. Echoes from loud tables bounced around the overly lit room. Mariana's sneakers stuck to the floor. Lunchtime was chaos. And chaos meant that teachers wouldn't notice anyone selling candy.

Blending in with the crowd, Mariana walked to her usual table near the middle of the cafeteria. She pulled her lunch from her backpack and started eating. Soon enough, Dawn came over and sat across the table.

"Hey," Dawn said. "You better than you were this morning?"

"Yeah," Mariana said. "I just got something I need to take care of after school."

She darted her eyes around, looking for suspicious teachers. Then, she leaned in closer to Dawn.

"You know anyone who wants to buy five caramel apple pops?" Mariana asked. "Like, right now?"

Dawn raised an eyebrow.

"You in a hurry?" Dawn asked.

Mariana nodded and took a drink from her water bottle. That was the only information Dawn needed. She looked around the cafeteria, scouting. And then a familiar smile graced her face, one of those smiles that Mariana had seen since they were little kids. That *I'll handle it* type of smile.

"I'll be right back," Dawn said.

Dawn walked over to a table of sixth graders. She smiled and sat down. She talked to the ringleader of the bunch, and then she stood and left, returning to her seat across from Mariana.

"Well," Mariana said, "what did you say to them?"

"Give it a minute," Dawn said.

Mariana didn't have the patience to wait a minute, but she didn't have a choice. Besides, Dawn usually came through.

As Mariana looked over to the table of sixth graders, she

saw one of them stand up and walk timidly toward Mariana's table.

"Told ya," Dawn said.

The sixth grader's pace slowed as he neared the table. Dawn subtly motioned toward Mariana.

"Uh, hey," the sixth grader muttered. "Can I get five?"

Mariana looked over her shoulder, checked for teachers, and slid five caramel apple pops across the table.

"Five bucks," Dawn said.

The sixth grader pulled out a five from his pocket and handed it to Mariana and scampered back to his table, thrilled to share his newfound wealth.

"Thanks," Mariana said.

"I got you," Dawn said.

The lunch bell rang, triggering a mass exodus from the cafeteria. Dawn grabbed her tray and maneuvered her legs out of the cafeteria table.

"See you last period," Dawn said.

Mariana's eyes shifted to the back door of the cafeteria.

"Not today," Mariana said.

"What do you mean?" Dawn asked.

"Don't worry about it," Mariana said. "I just have something to take care of. And it can't wait until after school."

Dawn shook her head and smiled before leaving the table, blending in with the crowd.

Mariana went to Spanish. While Señora Vasquez rambled on about the future tense, Mariana's eyes watched the clock. Five minutes left. Her leg started to twitch. She'd never skipped a class before.

The bell rang. Mariana grabbed her backpack and merged with the hallway traffic. She had a short window of time before the crowd thinned, and she needed to get out before that happened. As she walked through the hallway, she saw the back door. A teacher was posted up near the door, but he seemed focused on talking to a student about math homework. Mariana gripped her backpack straps to keep her hands from trembling. Keeping her eyes forward, she walked calmly to the door. She stood still and looked at the teacher. He didn't see her. Mariana nudged the door open and slid out, gently closing the door behind her.

She leaned against the brick building, waiting for a teacher to chase after her. But the door remained closed. And the seventh period bell rang.

Mariana checked her watch. She only had a half hour. She sprinted away from the school building and dashed down the sidewalk.

By the time she got to the boutique, the owner was packing up. Mariana blasted through the door. The bell rang, snapping the owner to attention.

"We close in five minutes, honey," the owner said.

Mariana stopped and caught her breath. She hadn't run that far that fast since last track season.

"I only need a minute," Mariana said. "I know exactly what I want."

The owner eyed Mariana, and then returned to her post behind the desk.

"I'll be here when you're ready," the owner said.

Mariana walked toward a table in the middle of the shop. Earrings and necklaces and bracelets, disorganized and eclectic. Her eyes darted from one piece of jewelry to the next.

And then she saw it. A thin silver chain with a silver heart. Just like the one from the picture. Just like the one Dad gave her on their wedding day. Just like the one that Mom had to sell to make rent when Dad got laid off from the factory and they had to move out of their house. And then into an apartment with government assistance.

"Will that be all, honey?" the owner asked.

Mariana nodded and placed the necklace on the counter. She saw the price flash across the register. Removing her wallet from her backpack, she placed a large stack of dollar bills on the counter.

"Looks like you've been saving up for something special," the owner said. "Would you like it gift wrapped?" the owner asked.

Her hands flew around the small necklace with ornate gift wrap and a glittery ribbon. Mariana thanked the owner and picked up the package. It felt so delicate in her hands.

When Mariana opened the door to her apartment, Mom was sitting in the kitchen drinking tea. Mariana put her backpack by the front door. She walked by the picture of Mom smiling. The thin silver chain with a silver heart dangled from her neck.

"Happy birthday, Mom," Mariana said.

Mom's eyes, heavy from the day, brightened as the gift appeared on the table. She sat up straight, looking at her daughter. Really looking at her. Mom opened the gift, meticulously unwrapping each corner. As she opened the box, she removed the necklace. And she smiled. Her first real smile in a very long time.

The Lunchroom

Oregon

Jamal dumped the entire contents of the brown paper bag on the cafeteria table. One cheese sandwich. One apple. One juice box. Two graham crackers. And three pieces of candy that read *fun size*.

"How they gonna call this *fun size* when you can eat the whole thing in one bite?" Jamal asked. "They should call the huge ones *fun size*."

"Those are *king size*," Scotty said.

Jamal rolled his eyes and slapped the piece of candy onto the table.

"That's the wrong name too," Jamal said. "We all know that the queens have all the power. My mom sure does, anyway."

Scotty nodded before lowering his head to inspect the items from Jamal's lunch, analyzing them like pieces on a chess board. And for good reason: navigating the lunch room free trade market required more strategy than a chess match.

"You brought the usual items," Scotty said.

"Yeah, mom hasn't gone shopping in a while," Jamal said.

"Mine hasn't either," Scotty said.

Scotty lowered his eyes just enough for Jamal to understand.

"Let's see what you got," Jamal said.

Opening his brown paper bag, Scotty dumped out his contributions: a bag of pretzels, a peanut butter and jelly sandwich, a water bottle, and a banana. He pushed Scotty's food together with his own, creating a pile of tradable goods.

"It's not much," Jamal said, "but we can work with that."

Lunch had just started. Jamal and Scotty sat on the far end of the cafeteria with the other fifth graders. Fourth graders occupied the next row, while third graders took the seats closest to the door.

"What do you see out there?" Scotty asked.

Jamal's eyes moved quickly but efficiently from one table to the next.

"We've got chocolate pudding at Table Two," Jamal said. "Third grade."

"Think we could trade that for your graham crackers?" Scotty asked.

Jamal smiled. He grabbed the graham crackers and walked toward the third grader. Laughter and excited chatter echoed through the cafeteria. The familiar smell of cleaning supplies and burned food filled the room. Jamal weaved through the tightly packed tables, trying to look casual as he approached the third grade section.

"Hey, Bradley," Jamal said.

The third graders looked up at him with wide eyes.

"How many days in a row have you had that same old chocolate pudding stuff?" Jamal continued.

"Every day this month," Bradley said.

"I figured," Jamal said. "It probably gets pretty old and boring after a while."

"I guess," Bradley said.

Jamal nodded, putting on a show of wisdom and experience.

"It's probably like having a s'more without all the good parts," Jamal said. "Like the marshmallow. Or everyone's favorite part: the graham cracker."

"I sure do like graham crackers," Bradley said.

Jamal worked to contain his excitement. He didn't want to give away his hand too soon.

"You don't say," Jamal said. "Well, it just so happens that I have, not one, but *two* graham crackers in my lunch today. Fresh from the box."

Bradley's eyebrows shot upward. He slowly reached for his chocolate pudding, suddenly aware of how mundane it had become.

"I'd be willing to give you the graham crackers for that boring pudding mush," Jamal said.

"Really? You would?" Bradley asked.

"Of course," Jamal said. "It's the least I could do."

Bradley handed his chocolate pudding to Jamal, who handed his graham crackers to the third grader. Jamal nodded and smiled, assuring Bradley that it was a fair deal. Then, Jamal returned to his own table.

"Good one," Scotty said.

"Easy sell," Jamal said. "Now we need to flip this pudding."

"How much you thinking?" Scotty asked.

"A dollar, easy," Jamal said.

Scotty snatched the pudding and weaved his way over to a sixth grade table, far out of sight from Bradley at Table Two. He spotted Nick, a regular customer. A dependable starting point for Scotty.

"Nick!" Scotty said, patting him on the back.

"Hey, Scotty," Nick said. "You have anything good today?"

Scotty smiled, exaggerating his mannerisms.

"I sure do," Scotty said. "High-quality chocolate pudding. The good stuff. Real chocolate."

Nick looked around at his sixth grade friends and smirked. He reached into his pocket and pulled out a pile of dollar bills.

"How much you want for it?" Nick asked.

Scotty loved this part. Nick's mom worked for some big company. He always had cash. And he had no concept of value, no idea that he could buy this same cup of chocolate pudding for twenty-five cents at the corner store.

"Usually I'd take two dollars for something this valuable," Scotty said. "But for you, I'd cut that in half to a dollar."

"Sounds like a deal," Nick said.

He pulled a dollar from his pile and handed it to Scotty, who handed the chocolate pudding to Nick. He looked around the table at his sixth grade friends, reveling in his victory. Scotty held in his own smile until he sat down by Jamal.

"Good work, Scotty," Jamal said. "Just a few more and we're good."

"I'll take the apple," Scotty said. "You take the pretzels and the fun size candy bar."

"Sounds good," Jamal said. "We can eat the rest for our own lunch."

"Meet back here in five."

By the time they came back from their next round of hustling, they had acquired a total of five dollar bills. And they still had two sandwiches and a banana to split.

By the time the bell rang at the end of the day, they were both hungry. But they had a plan. Scotty met Jamal by the playground as usual. The sun hung low in the sky, another early autumn sunset. Orange and red leaves covered the sidewalk, damp from the morning rain.

"You ready?" Jamal asked.

"Let's get it," Scotty said.

The corner store was only two blocks from school. Kids who walked north usually stopped there to grab a pop or some candy for the rest of the journey. But Jamal and Scotty never had any spare cash.

Unless they could trade for some at lunch. And today was one of those days.

The bell rang as they walked into the corner store. They passed by the soda fountain, where the owner had managed to squeeze three small tables and chairs to create a hangout area.

"Hey, boys!" the owner. "Happy Friday."

A small, grainy television blared from behind the counter, the announcer shouting commentary in Arabic over a soccer game.

"What's up, Mr. Bashir?" Jamal said.

He walked to the middle of the store and leaned against the counter.

"What you watching?" Jamal asked.

"Football," Mr. Bashir said.

Jamal looked at Scotty and laughed.

"Man, that's not football," Jamal said. "That's soccer."

"In every other country, this is football," Mr. Bashir said. "The best, most popular sport in the world."

"It's weak, Mr. Bashir," Scotty said. "They can't even hit each other."

"Oh, but they do. They use physical contact with such tact. Not like that brutish, simple football you have here in the States," Mr. Bashir said.

"They can't even use their hands!" Jamal said.

Mr. Bashir shook his head and laughed. The same conversation happened every day after school when the boys came in. They rarely bought anything, but they were friendly. And Mr. Bashir enjoyed the banter.

And the boys appreciated it too. Mr. Bashir had owned the corner store since Jamal and Scotty could remember. So, basically since forever. He had moved here from Iraq with his brother a long time ago. Mr. Bashir had a wife and daughter back in Iraq. He used to, at least. He talked about them all the time. But they weren't here anymore.

"Are you boys buying anything today?" Mr. Bashir said. "Or are you just here to watch football?"

He smirked, sending a message that he didn't care how they answered. They were always welcome.

Jamal looked at Scotty, and then turned his head toward Mr. Bashir. Stuffing his hand in his pocket, Jamal pulled out five dollar bills and placed them on the counter.

"Three pops. The good stuff. Brand name," Jamal said. "And three muffins."

Mr. Bashir smiled. He put the money in the register and walked over to the heated window with the baked goods.

"Go grab your sodas," Mr. Bashir said. "What type of muffins would you like?"

Scotty ran back and grabbed three bottles of pop, while Jamal stayed with Mr. Bashir.

"I'll take a chocolate chip muffin," Jamal said.

"Blueberry for me!" Scotty shouted from the back of the store.

Mr. Bashir turned to Jamal.

"And the third?" he asked.

"That's your choice," Jamal said. "We're buying the third for you, Mr. Bashir."

Nearly dropping the metal tongs, Mr. Bashir stood up straight and looked at Jamal. Tears began to well in his eyes, but he forced them back down.

"For me?" Mr. Bashir asked. "Why for me?"

Scotty returned with three bottles of pop. He handed one to Jamal and one to Mr. Bashir.

"Well, you always have to put up with us kids coming in here every day and running through your store and talking all kinds of trash," Jamal said. "We just thought it would be cool to pay you back somehow."

"But only under one condition," Scotty said. "You have to eat with us at that table over there so we can convince you that American football is the *real* football."

Mr. Bashir threw his head back and laughed. He grabbed a muffin and walked over to one of the small tables by the soda fountain. The small table held three pop bottles and three muffins without room for much else.

Jamal leaned in, resting his head on his hands, as if this argument was going to be easy.

"I mean, like, they don't even wear pads in soccer," Jamal said.

"Exactly," Mr. Bashir said. "Because soccer players are *tougher* than American football players."

Jamal and Scotty laughed through bites of muffins and drinks of pop. Then, Scotty leaned back in his chair and looked at Mr. Bashir with a serious face.

"Hey, Mr. Bashir," he said. "Did you play soccer back home?"

The Hustle

Pennsylvania

Jeremiah cut through the grass. Taking the predetermined cement pathways made things too obvious, too predictable. And besides, it was faster. Philadelphia's skyline towered above orange leaves and sparse trees. Fallen leaves crunched beneath his feet.

And then he felt it: gum on the bottom of his shoe.

Jeremiah stopped in the middle of the grass and analyzed the bottom of his new sneakers, finding freshly chewed pink gum.

He knew that he had already missed the train he wanted. The next one wouldn't come for a little while. Still, he wanted to hustle. If he missed another one, he'd be late for practice.

And late for practice meant *sprints*.

So he decided to forget the gum for now and worry about it when he got on the train.

He finally turned onto the pavement when he saw the entrance to the subway staircase. Then, he saw the three cards, faced down on the cardboard box. A guy behind the cards waved toward Jeremiah.

"Hey, young man," the guy said. "Step up, step up."

Jeremiah looked around, hoping that the man was talking to someone else.

"Step up and find the Red Queen," he continued. "Win twenty."

Jeremiah put his hand up in protest and moved to continue his walk. He didn't want to bet his own money on a game he'd probably lose. He didn't even think it was a game. More like a scam. But, if he won, he would have enough money to take *her* out to dinner.

"First game is free," the guy shouted. "No risk to win twenty."

Jeremiah's shoes nearly slipped on the cement as he stopped. He looked sideways at the makeshift card table. He felt his legs move toward the table until they were rooted in front of it. He looked down at the table and saw three cards, evenly spaced apart, creased longways down the center. The blue card backs contrasted against the pale cardboard.

The man behind the table controlled his sly smile. He lifted the middle card to reveal the Red Queen. Jeremiah nodded in recognition.

As the Red Queen lowered, Jeremiah's eyes zoned in. He knew that he had to block out any momentary distraction that would divert his eyes. The man behind the counter began to switch the face-down cards around. Jeremiah kept his focus on the hidden Red Queen. The three cards swirled around in a predictable figure-eight pattern, making it easy for Jeremiah to track his target card.

Jeremiah thought the cards would have moved faster. Or, maybe he was getting *really* good at this game.

The man slowed his figure-eight pattern and placed the three cards on the table. Jeremiah's confidence swelled.

"Well, my man," the guy said. "Where's the Red Queen?"

Jeremiah pointed at the left card. He tried hard to conceal his pride. The man behind the table flipped the left card and tossed it on the table: Red Queen.

He threw his hands up and spun around, amazed at Jeremiah's advanced ability to track the proper card. He reached into his pocket and slapped a twenty dollar bill on the table. Jeremiah grabbed at it.

But the man behind the table left his palm on the bill.

"You know, young man," the guy said. "Leave this twenty on the table. Add another twenty. Turn your forty into eighty. Easy money."

Jeremiah smiled to hide his hesitation. He knew the smart move: take the twenty and go. But that last round was so easy. Predictable and slow.

Jeremiah left the twenty on the table, reached for his wallet, and set another twenty down. He crossed his arms and nodded his head, confident that he would double his money and be on his way.

"Alright, playin' forty to win eighty," the guy said.

The man behind the table showed the Red Queen to Jeremiah and placed the card on the left. Jeremiah fixated his attention on the Red Queen's blue card back. The cards began to rotate in the same, slow, figure-eight pattern. But, then, the speed increased. One card flipped over another. And then another over another. And then another. Two cards disappeared beneath the same hand before one appeared to the left and another to the right. Jeremiah tracked the card that maintained the same trajectory as the Red Queen. But, then two other cards did the same disappearing act before emerging on the same side.

Suddenly, the three cards sat motionless on the table, as if they'd never moved.

"Well, my man," the guy said. "Where's the Red Queen?"

Jeremiah froze. He had been tracking a card that now stood in the middle. At least he thought it had been that card. Or maybe it was the right one. Definitely wasn't the left. Unless it was.

Having talked himself too far into thought, he reverted and pointed toward the middle card.

"You sure?" the guy asked.

Jeremiah nodded, convincing mostly himself that this was a confident decision.

"Yeah," Jeremiah said.

The man behind the table shrugged his shoulders and flipped the card: Red Five.

Jeremiah's head dropped. And so did his confidence.

"Come on, man" Jeremiah said, knowing that the man behind the table would hear no rebuttal.

"If you got twenty," the guy said, "play for your money back."

He smirked at Jeremiah, who began to get the feeling that he had been hustled. Hard to prove, but highly likely. He had a feeling that, no matter which card he picked, the Red Queen wasn't there at all.

And now he just felt foolish.

He *knew* that he'd been hustled.

Jeremiah waved off the offer and stepped away from the table. His energy had been depleted. He should have known that was a hustle. He was too street smart for that. But, maybe the man behind the counter was more street smart.

A gust of wind blew leaves through the park. Jeremiah ducked into the subway staircase, his sneakers echoing as he trotted down the stairs. The gum on the bottom of his shoe stuck to the cement. He hoped he hadn't missed the train.

As he rounded the corner, he saw the train already there, stationary with open doors. Jeremiah's sneakers shuffled quickly. He felt leaves on the bottom of his shoes, crunching and slipping with each step. He slid into the train as the doors began to close.

The train felt empty. Jeremiah found a seat near the door; he didn't have far to go. As he sat, he lifted his shoe up to work on gum removal. As his shoe flipped, he noticed a bill stuck to his sole. Gum snapped as he pulled the bill.

"A twenty," Jeremiah said.

The Bully

Rhode Island

Naomi slunk into her desk chair. Unlike most students, she wanted the school day to keep going, an endless session of math problems and English readings and science projects. She wanted the clock to freeze.

It wasn't that she loved school. Actually, Naomi *didn't* love school. She didn't mind the work or the content. She got decent grades and everything.

No, it wasn't school she disliked. It was the people at school she didn't like.

Well, not *all* of the people at her school, exactly. Just a few people. Really, just one person.

Allie.

Naomi tried to avoid her at all costs, but their lockers were right next to each other. Inevitably, no matter how hard she tried, Naomi ran into Allie every day after school. And it was *never* positive.

"Homework tonight," the teacher said. "Questions one through seventeen."

A collective groan rumbled through the classroom.

"And remember, tomorrow is the last day to turn in the

179

permission slip," the teacher continued.

As Naomi watched the clock, wishing it would stop, she knew that an encounter with Allie was only a few minutes away. The minute hand landed on the three. The bell rang, sending a shockwave of fear through Naomi's heart.

Students jumped from their chairs and flung backpacks on shoulders and dashed from the room. But Naomi took her time. She strolled out of class, hoping that Allie was one of those people who sprinted to her locker and then exited the building. Weaving through the crowded hallway, Naomi tried her best to remain invisible, to remain anonymous.

She saw her locker through the crowd. No one was around it. Exhaling, Naomi approached the lock.

Get in, get out, she thought.

She spun the lock and opened the locker door. She grabbed her novel for English class and her history textbook to accompany the gargantuan math book that already took up too much backpack space.

Naomi thought she was free. But, as Naomi closed her locker, Allie appeared, hovering by her own locker, an unshakable presence.

"Why do you wear your hair like that?" Allie asked.

Her lips curled into a devilish grin. She opened her locker and nudged Naomi out of the way.

"Because I like it this way," Naomi said.

"Well, you should think about getting a haircut," Allie said. "Or maybe dying it a different color."

Naomi's pulse quickened. Her body temperature increased, sending heat to her face. She scanned her mind, searching for the perfect rebuttal, the perfect comeback. But nothing came. Instead, Allie closed her locker, smirked at Naomi, and walked away.

With the weight of her backpack and humiliation lingering, Naomi leaned against her own locker for support. No one else seemed to notice. Or maybe they noticed, but didn't care. Or maybe they cared, but were too cowardly to step in. Either way, Naomi wanted to puke. Or punch a hole through her locker. Or collapse to the floor and cry.

After regaining what remained of her composure, Naomi stepped into the thinning crowd and emerged from the school building. It was one of those rare sunny days in winter where the sun had burned off the sea fog that typically engulfed the town. Naomi squinted, shielding her eyes, unfamiliar with the sun. She turned by the soccer field and continued her stroll down the sidewalk.

Why does she have to be so mean? Naomi wondered. *It's not like I ever did anything to make her mad.*

Naomi had, in fact, done the opposite. She had gone out of her way to stay out of Allie's way. Yet, somehow, Allie had spent the entire school year using Naomi as a verbal punching bag.

And Naomi's thick skin had worn thin.

Turning the corner, Naomi decided that she needed a quick mood booster, so she stopped at the ice cream shop. Kids from school rarely went there. Maybe it was just far enough away that it lost its convenience. Or maybe kids were focused on other after school activities. Naomi didn't have much planned, like, ever. So a spontaneous ice cream stop without the risk of running into any kids from school was always a good idea.

Thoughts of mint chocolate chip and double chocolate brownie and salted caramel swirled through Naomi's mind.

But as she stepped into the line, her mind stopped, frozen

with panic.

Allie stood there, waiting to order. An older woman stood next to her, probably her mom.

Naomi shifted her eyes and pretended to be overly interested in the twelve flavors on the menu. She could feel Allie's glare.

Finally, Naomi couldn't avoid it. She moved her attention to Allie, who averted her eyes.

Here comes the venom, Naomi thought, waiting for a poisonous comment from Allie.

But it never came.

Standing in line, Naomi noticed a difference in Allie. She looked almost *nervous*. The domineering persona, the spiteful, vindictive attitude that Allie showed at school was nowhere to be found in the ice cream line.

"What are you going to order?" Allie's mom asked.

Allie shifted her stance.

"Maybe a double scoop of chocolate," Allie said.

"Honey, you don't need a double scoop," Allie's mom said. "You're getting a little thick around the hips."

Allie seemed to shrink. Naomi thought she saw Allie glance in her direction, but maybe she imagined it.

"And you really shouldn't get chocolate," Allie's mom continued. "It'll bring out even more zits on your face than you have already."

This time, Allie *did* look at Naomi. And Naomi felt sorry for Allie. No matter how mean Allie had been to Naomi, no girl deserved to have their mother treat them like that. Naomi's pity began to shift into something more actionable. Something that resembled defensiveness. And then, she felt herself take a step forward in line. And she felt her voice begin to rumble.

"I was thinking of getting a double scoop of chocolate,

myself," Naomi said.

Allie's mom whipped her head around and glared at Naomi. Allie snuck a look at Naomi that resembled gratitude.

Allie's mom heard her phone ring, so she dug into her purse and grabbed it. She answered, aggressively directing the person on the other end. She paid for Allie's ice cream, and then covered the phone's mouthpiece.

"I have to head back to the office," Allie's mom said to her daughter. "You can walk home from here."

Allie nodded, a nod that expressed relief and disappointment. She slowly walked toward the door. Naomi grabbed her own cup of ice cream and followed Allie onto the sidewalk.

"Hey, Allie," Naomi said. "Do you want to stay and eat your ice cream with me?"

Allie turned around and looked at Naomi, unsure how serious to take the offer. Naomi walked to a small, two-person table outside the ice cream shop and sat down. She motioned to the other chair. Allie slowly smiled and sat down across from Naomi.

"So," Naomi said, "how's that double scoop?"

The Collection

South Carolina

The car pulled up along the curb. The man and his two boys got out of the car and walked up to the table beneath the shade of a broad oak tree. A brief refuge from the summer sun, the shade did little for the intense humidity.

"Three lemonades, please," the man said.

Lucy smiled, showing all of her teeth and the spot where one had recently fallen out. Twenty-five cents from the tooth fairy.

Reaching into the cooler, Lucy removed the pitcher of lemonade from ice. The pitcher dripped with melted water, cooling Lucy's hands. She filled three paper cups with lemonade and set them on the table.

"Three dollars, please," Lucy said.

The man's eyes widened just long enough for Lucy to catch it. A dollar per cup was a steep price increase, but she knew the man couldn't back away now. Besides, her sign stated the price in big, bold letters. He reluctantly handed three bills to Lucy, who accepted them graciously before stuffing them into a jar half-full with cash.

"Thank you, ma'am," the man said.

Lucy smiled again, waving to the family as they pulled away from the curb.

The screen door opened and Grandma emerged from the house. She walked slowly up to the lemonade stand and took a seat. Her back was bent, her knees stiff with age.

"Looks like you've had a steady stream of customers today," Grandma said. "I'll bet you've got something special you're saving up for."

"I sure do," Lucy said.

Grandma leaned in, expecting Lucy to tell her more. But Lucy returned to her newest pitcher of lemonade, squeezing lemon juice and mixing it with water and sugar. Grandma placed her hands on her knees and hoisted herself from the chair.

"Well, I'll leave you to it," Grandma said.

Lucy smiled at Grandma and continued making more lemonade. Grandma disappeared back into the house.

She wouldn't understand, Lucy thought.

Over the years, Lucy had listened to Dad and Grandma talk about giving to those who needed it, sharing with those who had less. But she had *seen* Dad act differently. His actions didn't match his words. He collected money. He never gave it to people. He even let the collection plate pass him by every Sunday at church.

"Those lazy people on welfare just take my tax dollars," Dad would say.

"People these days just take and take and take," Grandma would say.

"Everyone is always looking for a handout," Dad would say. "It's a shame that the government gives it to them."

But Lucy also noticed that Dad and Grandma accepted

185

money from the government when they were going through tough times. It was confusing to watch. So, a few months ago, Lucy decided to make her own decision. She would share with people who needed it. No matter what.

A group of younger kids walked by. Two of them carried baseball gloves. They bought a few cups of lemonade and continued their stroll.

Lucy mixed more lemonade. As the wooden spoon churned in the pitcher, she wondered how Alex's lemonade stand was going. His street wasn't as busy as Lucy's, but there were more kids on his block that might stop by. Five blocks the other direction, Annette was probably raking in dollar bills. The bus stop was right next to her house.

As the day got hotter, car after car stopped and purchased a few cups. Lucy's prime location on the corner of two neighborhood streets guaranteed a steady stream of cars on the way home from work, and a few walkers on their way from the bus stop. Dollar bills exchanged for fresh-squeezed lemonade. And on a hot day like this, people would be craving a cold drink.

Eventually, the sun dipped behind the house, providing even more shade on the lawn.

"Supper time," Grandma hollered from the porch.

"Be right in," Lucy said.

She packed up her cooler with the remaining lemons and the last full pitcher. She grabbed her jars of cash and her sign and took them inside.

Lucy sped through dinner, eating her entire plate before Grandma and Dad had even loaded theirs. She dashed into the kitchen and cleaned her plate and some of the cooking dishes.

"Can I go over to Alex's for a little bit?" Lucy asked.

Dad looked at Grandma, who had just stuffed a dinner roll into her mouth.

"Sure," Dad said, "but only for a little bit. Be back before it gets too dark."

Lucy smiled, showing her lost tooth gap. She ran into her room and grabbed her jars of cash. When she got outside, she jumped on her bike and put her jars in the basket. She pedaled hard for five blocks and found Alex waiting on his porch. Annette was already there.

"Hey, guys," Lucy said. "How much did we get today?"

Alex dumped his cash onto the cracked cement walkway. Annette did the same.

"Looks good," Lucy said, adding her cash to the pile. "Let's start counting."

Dollar bills flicked between hands as the friends counted in silence. Finally, they came up with a final number.

"That should get you there, Alex," Annette said.

"Especially with the money from yesterday," Lucy said.

Alex cast his eyes downward at the money.

"Are you sure you want to do this?" Alex asked. "You both earned more than I did today."

"Of course!" Lucy said. "Annette and I already have bikes. If we can use our resources to get you one, think about how much better things will be for *all* of us."

Lucy thought about the possibilities. If Alex had a bike, all three of them could ride around the neighborhood. They could ride all the way to the pool, to the park, to the store, to each other's houses. It wasn't simply a benefit for *Alex*. It helped the whole group.

"But it's not your fault that I don't have a bike," Alex said. "My parents just don't have the money for one right now."

Lucy smiled at Annette.

"Of course it's not *our* fault that you don't have a bike," Lucy said. "It's not *your* fault either."

"But it is our responsibility as friends to help you out," Annette said.

Alex lifted his eyes. Lucy thought he was holding back tears, but she couldn't quite tell.

"With the amount of money you raised by yourself today, you could save up to buy your own bike," Alex said.

"And what would I do with another bike?" Lucy asked.

A light breeze swept away some of the humidity. Lucy saw a dollar bill flicker, so she took the pile of money and stuffed it into a jar. Once the jar was full, she handed it to Alex. He nodded, still forcing back tears. He wanted to thank them, but he couldn't get the words out.

"Besides," Lucy said, "after you get a bike, we'll use our next batch of cash to get something for one of us. Or maybe something for the whole group."

"We'll keep using our resources to make us *all* better," Annette said.

The Mountains

South Dakota

The woman got out of the old truck and stepped onto the concrete. The amount of cars and motorhomes was unlike anything she had ever seen in real life. Or anything she ever cared to see. The cement felt false beneath her thin-soled shoes. She preferred dirt roads, grass paths. This yellow-lined concrete seemed so permanent, so imposing.

Following dozens of signs and arrows, she walked down the path, herded into a mob of tourists from everywhere, hundreds of bodies, weighed down by decades of fake burgers and high fructose corn syrup and selective immobility. The woman wove between them with nervous grace.

Stone pillars lined the walkway. Each pillar hoisted a flag from each of the fifty states. She recognized a few. When she came to the South Dakota flag, a strange shudder fired through her nerves.

Then, as she moved down the path, she saw it: Mount Rushmore. Four giant rock faces carved into the side of a mountain in the Black Hills. Former United States presidents whose legends had grown as inflated with time as the mountain had changed over centuries.

189

"Wow!" a young boy shouted, tugging at his mom's coat.

Near them, a middle-aged man gasped. He wobbled his way forward, trying to get a better view with his binoculars.

Everyone seemed to be in awe, inspired by the grandeur of the imposing figures, their legendary profiles casting shadows over the land.

But the woman felt something different. She felt sad. Her spirit deflated.

"They came in and scarred the mountain," her grandmother used to say. "Something so beautiful, stamped with something so terrible."

The Black Hills were sacred to the Sioux, to her people. A place where they could find peace and harmony and ritual. In 1868, the U.S. government promised the Black Hills to the Sioux for all time. But then they found gold and revoked that promise, capturing the sacred land and massacring its people. Then, to stamp its control, the U.S. government commissioned that four of its most famous faces would scar the mountain, overlooking the land that they claimed. Four faces that represented leadership to some, but desecration to others.

Two of the faces owned slaves, treating hundreds of humans like their own personal property. One of the faces was assassinated because he ended slavery. The final face propagated the idea of controlling other lands and peoples through imperialism.

In fact, now that the woman looked at Mount Rushmore, she realized that it was the most American symbol that America could create for itself.

"Look at how big his nose is!" a little girl shouted.

"How'd they get up there?" a little boy asked.

A park ranger walked over to the curious kids and knelt down to face them

"Well, that's a great question," he said. "Dozens of people had to hang over the mountainside on ropes and blow up pieces of the mountain with dynamite."

The little boy's eyes widened as he looked at his sister.

"And then, they took chisels and carved out the details," the park ranger continued.

A small crowd began to gather around the park ranger, who was embracing the interest.

"After the project started," the park ranger continued, "President Franklin D. Roosevelt decided to give the project federal funding as part of an initiative to put Americans back to work during the Great Depression."

The woman felt her hand raise on its own, controlled by something far beyond her own mind, something ancestral. The park ranger looked up and smiled, pointing to the woman.

"Did the rightful owners of the land give their permission for this to happen?" the woman asked.

"Of course," the park ranger said. "The U.S. government controlled the land as part of its national parks program."

"Which they illegally took from the Lakota Sioux," the woman said. "So, did the Sioux give their permission to have their sacred land desecrated with the faces of their colonizers?"

The park ranger turned white. Whiter, anyway. He looked around at the crowd, which had grown quite large. No one spoke, each waiting for someone else to take on the question. Seconds passed silently. Or maybe it was minutes. Finally, a little girl stepped forward and looked at the woman.

"It's kind of like if someone took my favorite basketball on the playground, wrote their own name on it in big letters, and then said it was their basketball," the little girl said.

The woman knelt down to the little girl's level, but her eyes remained focused on the park ranger.

"It is very much like that," the woman said.

The woman stood and smiled at the stunned crowd. She nodded and continued her walk toward the mountain, toward the viewpoint. Leaning against the wooden fence, she looked into the stone eyes of the four white men that bulged from the mountainside.

"We won't stop fighting," she whispered. "You can scar our land. You can suppress our culture and our language. But we won't stop fighting."

A tear streamed down her face. It fell from her cheek and landed in the dirt, soaking into the earth, into the land that the woman would forever know as home.

The Singer

Tennessee

The bar was packed. All four floors of it. Ollie could see the neon lights from the bars across the street. Pinks and greens and yellows, cutting through the humid night air into the open windows.

He took another drink of water and stepped back onto the stage, blinded by the stage lights. As he looked into the crowd, all he saw were figures and shapes, but he could tell that the place was full. He sat down on his stool and placed the guitar on his leg. Behind him, the drummer and bass player tuned their instruments and got themselves ready to continue their set.

"We're back, everyone," Ollie said into the microphone. "Just had to get a quick drink of whiskey to keep these golden pipes going."

Ollie heard a few laughs from the crowd. A drunk woman screamed from somewhere in the back of the bar.

"Someone get her another drink," Ollie said.

The crowd laughed a little more this time. Ollie squinted his eyes and looked through the barrel of his curved ball cap bill. He always wore a baseball cap. He was a country singer, but he wasn't a cowboy. And he wasn't going to pretend like he was.

"Here's a new one that we're going to try out on y'all tonight," Ollie continued.

The drummer started playing a light rhythm. The bass player began a low baseline on his strings.

"We wrote this one a few weeks ago when we were missing some family back home," Ollie said. "When we're done, let us know what you think."

Ollie's smooth voice broke into the microphone and pumped out into the crowd, creating a cheer from the drunk voices on the dance floor and the tables upstairs. Ollie's left hand moved swiftly from a G chord to a C chord, and then back again, repeating the pattern until the chorus. A standard country music sound. Occasionally, he flicked the strings or muted them or gave them a little percussion, just for his own entertainment. But the high energy drums and the funky bass brought everyone out to the dance floor. And when the song finished, Ollie cozied up to the microphone again.

"So, what'd y'all think?" Ollie asked.

Through loud, indiscernible shouts, Ollie smiled at the positive feedback. Every crowd for the last few weeks had loved the song.

But, for Ollie, the song represented something less positive. A longing to be home.

After another hour, Ollie and his band stood and bowed to the audience, who had gotten progressively more drunk as the night went on. They stuffed twenty dollar bills into the open guitar case in front of the stage and cheered and hollered.

Finally, Ollie and his band went backstage and sat for a moment.

"They loved it," the drummer said. "Especially that new one you wrote."

"They sure did," Ollie said.

The drummer leaned forward and looked at Ollie.

"Doesn't that make you want to stay?" the drummer asked.

Ollie smiled. He knew the question was coming. But he had made up his mind. Or at least he *thought* he had.

"I just can't put my family through this anymore, man," Ollie said. "I'm playing every night at bars in Nashville while my wife and kids are back home waiting around for me. And what are they waiting for?"

"For you to make it big, man!" the drummer said. "And you're almost there. You heard the crowd tonight. It's only a matter of time before your agent gets you that big record deal."

Ollie shook his head and stood up, pacing around the small room.

"We've been saying that for two years," Ollie said. "What if we have to wait for two more?"

"So what?" the drummer said. "What's two more years for a lifetime of fame?"

"My daughter will be five by then," Ollie said. "I'll have damn near missed her entire childhood. And for what? To get famous for a minute?"

The drummer shook his head. He stood and left the room. The bass player leaned against the wall and smiled. He had enjoyed watching the same argument take place after every show for the last two years. And it always ended the same way. Right back in the same bar the next night, playing another two-hour set.

But tonight, Ollie decided something needed to change.

He packed up his precious guitar in its felt-lined case. He

helped his band get their gear packed away. He shook hands with the bass player and the drummer. And then, he walked through the back alley to his car. Popping open the trunk, he placed his guitar down gently next to the duffel bag full of clothes and the few important trinkets he had acquired after two years in the city.

As he pulled away from the parking lot, he took one last look at the long street. And then, he slowly accelerated, cutting through the humid night air. He would be home by sunrise. Home for good with his daughters in his arms and his wife by his side. Long after the neon lights had faded.

The Reporter

Texas

Glasses rested on the end of his nose. He stared at the screen, waiting for the words to flow through his mind and flow to his fingers and *click-clack* the keyboard, creating the perfect story.

He'd been waiting for a half hour. So far, no magic.

So, he swiveled his desk chair around and walked through the small maze of cubicles to the coffee machine.

"Farouk," the editor said. "How's that story about rising crime rates going?"

"It's going fine," Farouk said. "I've completed most of the interviews I'll need. I'm just having a hard time getting my first words in order."

The editor patted Farouk on the shoulder, unaware that he nearly caused Farouk to spill his coffee.

"It'll happen," the editor said. "But I need that story on my desk by the end of the day."

The editor turned to leave. Farouk looked at the clock above the editor's head and held back a wince. Lingering for a moment, Farouk hustled back to his computer with his half-full coffee cup. He squinted his eyes, knowing that the action would make words emerge more efficiently.

But nothing happened.

He couldn't understand why, either. Farouk had interviewed the police chief twice. He had taken notes of the audio recording. He interviewed a city council member, the leader of an organization that advocated for alternative crime prevention methods, two convicted felons, an average homeowner, a small business owner, and a data analyst for the city's Department of Justice. Farouk had too much information. But he couldn't write the first sentence.

The editor wanted him to write a piece about how the rise in crime rates was driven by a reduction in the police budget. The angle would play well with the newspaper's audience. And the headline would all but guarantee clicks, which would jack up the newspaper's presence in search engines. And it would generate more advertising money for the newspaper.

Looking at the pages and pages of notes from his interviews, Farouk tried to shape the story in his mind. He tried to piece together segments and statistics and common observations from all of his sources that would point to the correlation between reduced police budgets and rising crime rates.

"It does feel like we're operating on such a tight budget these days," the police chief said.

"If we would just put more money in the police department, these criminals would get scared," the homeowner said.

The quotes were there, scattered throughout the organized notes and recordings. Still, Farouk couldn't bring himself to write the first sentence. But, the more he stared at the blank page, the more he began to understand.

The rest of the story wasn't lining up.

"Police budgets in our city *and* our state have risen steadily for the past two decades," the data analyst from the Department of Justice said. "We've hired more police, acquired more equipment, and amplified police technology more in the last decade than we did during the War on Drugs."

"Public records show that, with ballooning police budgets, we see an increase in *arrests*, but not necessarily a drop in crime," the activist said.

As Farouk sifted through more notes, he realized that the simple narrative his editor wanted wasn't lining up. And things continued to get murkier.

"We didn't care about the police in our neighborhood," one felon said. "Actually, some of the police were in on it with us."

"There were *so* many police cars rolling through our block," another felon said. "But they weren't putting food on our table. I didn't care about them. I just had to find ways around it."

"If we had more investment in early childhood education, family planning, food accessibility, and *actual* job opportunities, we'd see a dramatic drop in crime," the activist said.

The city council member ran on a similar agenda, but hadn't yet put any of those plans into practice.

Sifting through more notes, Farouk started to see so many inconsistencies. Too many to ignore. And he knew what he needed to do. He swiveled his chair around again. This time, he bypassed the cubicle maze and went to the editor's office.

"Hey," Farouk said, knocking as he opened the door.

"You got that story for me?" the editor asked.

Farouk shook his head and stepped farther into the office.

"That's what I came to talk to you about," Farouk said. "I need to take a different angle."

The editor scrunched his face up and looked sternly at Farouk.

"Not something we can do," the editor said. "We need a story about the correlation between decreased police budgets and rise in crime rates."

"But that's not the story that I'm getting from my interviews, nor is that what the data is showing us," Farouk said. "I need to take a different angle for this story to be ethical."

The editor stood and walked around his desk. He sat on the front of it and crossed his arms.

"Farouk," the editor said, "I know you've only been here a few months. Let me tell you how things work around here. We write a certain type of story. Our audience sees that headline. They can't help but click it. They share it on social media. They're friends who think exactly like they do are going to click it, and then share it. That story is going to spread in the social media echo chamber for a handful of hours. We get more views, which translates to more ad dollars."

He raised an eyebrow, waiting for a sign that Farouk understood the process. But Farouk's face expressed bewilderment.

"So you're going to write the story the way I tell you," the editor continued.

Farouk forced himself to snap from his trance of disbelief. He looked at the newspaper's logo emblazoned on the wall. Below it, the newspaper's tagline read: *Tell the truth*.

Farouk stepped toward the editor.

"So, you don't want an honest, ethical story?" Farouk asked.

The editor smirked and adjusted his crossed arms.

"I want a story that our target audience will click on," the editor said.

"So, you want me to lie?" Farouk asked.

"I want a story that our target audience will click on," the editor repeated.

Farouk's eyes traveled back to the newspaper's motto. And then he allowed himself to smirk.

"Got it," Farouk said.

The editor smiled and sauntered back to his desk chair, lifting his feet onto the desk. Farouk weaved through the cubicles and returned to his own desk. But he didn't sit. Instead, he grabbed his computer, a few notebooks, and pens. He stuffed everything into his bag and slung it over his shoulder.

As he walked by the editor's office window, Farouk simply waved. He took the elevator down to the ground level. Walking through the lobby, Farouk emerged into the warm afternoon sun, free to tell the truth.

The Telescope

Utah

The boy crawled through the window onto the roof. Closing the window behind him, he placed his foot on the plywood board so the roof wouldn't creak and wake up his parents. It was dark outside and the sky was clear. Snow covered the ground below the apartment. The boy pulled his coat around his neck and tugged his knit cap below his ears.

Walking across the roof, careful not to step on any weak spots, he moved over to the ledge and sat on a bench. It wasn't an *actual* bench. The boy had made it out of two cinder blocks and a long wooden board. It didn't look good. But it worked.

"Look at the beautiful sky," he said.

The boy didn't have many people to talk to. He knew that no one was awake this late, so he felt comfortable voicing his thoughts out loud, just above a whisper so his parents wouldn't hear.

His eyes traveled upward. The stars twinkled, just like the song his mom used to sing. He lived far enough into the mountains that skies weren't dulled by light pollution.

"Here we go," the boy said.

He took the cover off of the telescope and placed his eye

onto the eyepiece. Adjusting the focus and the aperture, he stared at a planet millions of miles away. He looked and looked and looked.

Finally, as he moved his eye away from the telescope and laid on his back and looked up. No telescope. Just his own two eyes.

Thousands or millions of stars and planets and galaxies.

He wondered what else was out there. If so much happened on little, tiny Earth, what was going on throughout all the planets in all the galaxies?

The boy already knew about Earth. Mostly water. A lot of land. Humans were the dominant species. He hadn't seen much of Earth, but his parents told him a lot about it. And he watched the news with them. He knew the world was a scary place.

They told him that crime was everywhere, and the news said that crime was on the rise. People just hurt other people for no reason. Walking down the street, someone could get robbed, kidnapped, hit by a car. They said it happened all the time. In the movies he watched, the boy saw how cruel kids were to each other. Kids made fun of each other, stuffed them in lockers, beat up other kids for no reason. People starved from lack of food. People didn't have homes, so they had to sleep on the street, even in the snow. World leaders bombed other countries just to take their resources. People were degraded because of their religion, or their race, or their nationality.

No wonder his parents never let him play outside. It was dangerous out there. Even schools were dangerous. That's what the news said, anyway. That's why his parents home schooled him.

The boy allowed his vision to drift upward again to the

canvas of stars in the sky. So many other worlds out there that circled around so many other suns.

"Which one of those planets is actually peaceful?" he said. "Which one of those places finally did it?"

He sat up and placed his eye back to the telescope. Focusing his lens, he searched the sky, stopping momentarily on each star he found, each planet.

"Or maybe none of these planets have done it," he said. "Maybe it's universal nature to want total domination, to be mean to people."

He focused his attention on one star. It seemed so close in his telescope. So close he could almost touch it. But he knew that the light he saw from that star was thousands of years old. Things had probably changed a lot on the planets that surrounded that star in the last couple thousand years.

Things had certainly changed on Earth. For better, and for worse. But maybe in that solar system, things had changed for the better. Or maybe things were just like they were on Earth. Terrifying and scary and dangerous and getting worse all the time. Just like his parents said.

He leaned away from the telescope again. Sitting on the bench, he looked over the ledge of the apartment roof. A single street light illuminated the corner. It was late. No one was awake.

No one *should* have been, anyway.

He saw an old man trudging through the snow on the sidewalk. He was trying to cross the street, but his old legs had a hard time moving in the cold, and he seemed nervous about the ice on the ground. Then, the boy noticed a man, about his dad's age, come out from a small house. He reached for the old man's arm, bracing him as he crossed the street. Once the man guided him to safety, the old man smiled. His teeth flickered beneath the streetlight.

The old man disappeared into the shadow of the streets, while the younger man disappeared into his own house. A quick interaction. No one saw it. No one was *supposed* to see it. The news wouldn't report it. The boy's parents wouldn't talk about it at the dinner table.

But the boy saw it.

There was so much badness in the world. This he knew. But maybe, just maybe, there was goodness too.

Returning to the bench, he looked up. With his own two eyes, he could see the entirety of space without much detail. With a telescope, he could focus on one specific scene, but he would miss out on all the other scenes taking place at the exact same time.

But he had the power to choose where to look, to change the source of light his telescope received. Placing his eye to the viewfinder, he refocused his lens and wondered where to aim his attention.

The Date

The line was long, bending around the block. Elias couldn't decide if he was sweating from the late summer heat or from the nerves pulsating through his body. He needed to get inside the ice cream shop to cool him down.

Cora stood next to him. She blurred the line between close and closer. She was close enough to suggest interest, but far enough away to plant uncertainty in Elias's mind. But he had expected this. It was their first date, after all.

Actually, Elias was still unsure whether or not this counted as a date. He asked her out to ice cream. She agreed. It *seemed* like a date. At least it did to him. But he wasn't sure if she thought about it like that.

"A lot of people must like this place," Cora said. "I mean, this line is crazy."

"Yeah," Elias said. "It's pretty good. Have you ever been here before?"

"No I haven't," Cora said.

She saw the line ahead of her and noticed a few other couples holding hands and getting close.

Elias probably takes dates here all the time, she thought.

206

He had a reputation, after all. Every girl talked about him. He always seemed so cool. So confident. Maybe over-confident, or maybe that was just an image that had been projected onto him. But, with that smile, any girl would jump at the chance to stand in an ice cream line with him.

Cora looked down at her shoes, and then lifted her eyes to meet Elias's.

"I come here with my mom and little brother a lot," Elias said. "My little brother always pretends like he's making a big decision, but he always gets the same thing: chocolate chip."

Cora smiled. Elias didn't have the reputation of a family guy. But maybe there was more to him than his reputation. And his eyes and his biceps. And his perfect teeth. And his all-star football statistics. And his big-man-on-campus persona. And the fact that every girl in the junior class was obsessed with him.

"I just like the vibe of this place," he continued. "This old brick building used to be a market back in the 1800s. It almost got torn down back when my mom was a kid, but this ice cream shop bought it and saved it. Saved its story."

He looked at Cora to see if she was interested in what he was saying. He thought he saw her smile, but maybe she was pretending to be interested. He averted his eyes and glanced at his own shoes: throwback sneakers, untied and slightly scuffed.

I need to stop talking so much, Elias thought. *She doesn't care about the history of this building. She wants a smooth, funny guy, like all the cool guys in the movies.*

"I didn't know you were into history," Cora said. "I love history."

Elias's eyebrows shot up. Cora was in AP World History,

after all. She got really good grades and was in the honor society, and she did all kinds of community service. Maybe she really was interested in what he had to say.

"You didn't strike me as the type of guy who would like that stuff," Cora said.

"Oh yeah?" Elias said. "Why not?"

Cora dug her toe into the concrete.

"Well," she said, "I just assumed that, since you played football, you were only into sports and parties and girls and stuff."

Elias raised an eyebrow, amused at her assumptions. He held back a smile, proud to rise above the first impression.

"All the girls love you," Cora said. "I just thought it was for your looks."

Her face beamed red. Cora ducked her head, trying to hide her embarrassment.

I can't believe I just said that, she thought. *I basically just told him that I liked him.*

Elias couldn't hold his smile back any longer. He started laughing. Cora looked up at him and laughed too.

"What's so funny?" she asked.

"I appreciate your honesty," he said. "Can I be honest back?"

"Of course you can," she said.

Elias glanced over his shoulder to make sure no one else was listening.

"I don't talk to a lot of girls. I get really nervous," he said. "I've actually never been on a real date before."

Cora laughed, a real laugh that she couldn't control. She buried her head into his shoulder.

"You, Elias, the king of the school, have never been on a real date?" Cora said.

"I'm serious," Elias said. "I get too nervous. And I don't have time. Between football practice, AP English homework, maintaining straight A grades, taking care of my little brother after school, and working at the restaurant on the weekends, I just don't have time."

He's in AP English, Cora thought. *And he works? I had no idea.*

The line had moved quite a bit since they started diving into a real conversation, an honest conversation. They had taken incremental steps around the block. As if no time had passed at all, they found themselves at the font of the line.

Nervously, Elias motioned for Cora to order whatever she wanted. And then Elias ordered. At the counter, he paid for both of their ice creams and the server handed them each a cone with a single scoop of chocolate chip.

"So, to be honest," Elias said, "this is my first date."

Cora felt her face flush again. She tried to hold back the beaming smile that longed to escape.

"Well Elias," Cora said, "I'm really enjoying *our* first date."

The Museum

Virginia

The sun had hardly risen above the treeline, but the air was already thick with humidity. A thin fog sat beneath the symmetrical rows of oak trees that lined the long driveway. Cars would trickle in after an hour or so when the museum opened. Even though it wasn't the busy season, late summer still brought in plenty of tourists from other states who wanted to take tours and learn about what happened here. And it was Claire's job to tell them the story.

"We have a high school tour group for you this morning," the supervisor said.

His drawl seemed forced, something out of a bygone era. Claire could never decide if his silver hair was slicked back by pounds of grease, or by the humidity. Either way, it looked slimy.

"Make sure we give these kids a good show," he said.

He winked at Claire and adjusted his suit jacket. Claire smiled and nodded like she did every day. As the supervisor walked away, Claire grabbed her clipboard and left the big house, which served as the museum's main building.

Standing on the porch, her eyes scanned the panoramic view

of the old plantation. The property spanned in front of her in every direction, disappearing into the horizon. The big house towered above everything else, a monolith at the center of the property. Its columns evoked a sense of something ancient, a symbol of power and control, reminding Claire of something Roman. A few brick buildings dotted the landscape; a long time ago, each building was used for a different farming purpose. Fields sprawled in all directions. Two centuries ago, tobacco plants filled the fields, cultivated by 250 people, the descendants of captives from West Africa. Their former living quarters, cramped and made of wood, had been destroyed by time.

Claire had worked at the plantation museum for five years. She got the job right out of college. As an American History major, this was her dream job. She couldn't wait to expose the evils of slavery, the system that had propped up America's thriving capitalist society.

But when she arrived at the museum, her supervisor viewed things differently.

"Stick to the script," the supervisor said. "You might learn something."

Fresh out of college, Claire didn't have the experience to push back against the supervisor. He had been doing this for decades. Who was she to contradict such a seasoned veteran?

She pandered to the mostly white, mostly American audience members that flocked to the plantation day after day after day. Her speech centered around the family that owned the plantation.

"The family owned hundreds of acres in the plantation's glory days, a bustling, happy time," Claire said. "They used their wealth charitably, donating to honorable causes across

Virginia."

Yet they thought that they could own human beings, Claire thought.

She would look around at all the tourists, who smiled and nodded, reveling in their own shields of charity.

"After fighting for America's freedom during the Revolution," Claire continued, "one of the sons of this plantation even became a Senator."

And he advocated for the expansion of slavery into America's newest states, Claire thought.

Every time she said this, a male tourist would raise his eyebrows, amazed at the power that the title of Senator held.

"The family maintained ownership of the property since it was founded in 1659," Claire said.

Property that they stole from the hundreds of indigenous people that they killed, Claire thought.

"They must have been some of the first people here," a tourist always said.

Claire shook her head slightly, but always returned to the smile and nod. She had to stick to the script. And if she didn't, she would be looking for employment elsewhere. But her supervisor was old. If she could hold on a little longer, maybe she could become the supervisor and make the changes that the museum needed.

Just a little longer.

"During the War between the States, the family offered up their home to the brave Confederate troops that fought for their rights," Claire said.

That line crushed her soul every time she had to say it.

I can't believe that Americans admire these people who rebelled against their country just to keep humans in bondage, Claire thought.

"What happened to the plantation after the Civil War?" someone always asked.

"The Union granted this land back to the original family," Claire said. "The family allowed its slaves to stay as free people, and they paid them for their work."

Paid them pennies on the dollar, Claire thought. *The family kept these workers in so much debt that they could never leave. And passed laws that made leaving a crime punishable by enslavement.*

And the script never mentioned any enslaved person by name. Ever.

Five years. The same script. The same questions. The same unspoken thoughts and unsaid historical accuracies. The same pandering to her audience's comfortability.

The tour group of high school kids has already gathered by the flagpole in front of the big house. Claire approached quickly, smiling extra wide to foster a sense of excitement to the teenagers that looked less than thrilled to be at the museum this early.

"Welcome!" Claire said. "I'm so glad y'all could join us out here today on such a lovely morning."

She never said *y'all* in her everyday speech, but it played to the audience and the atmosphere.

Fifteen high schoolers strolled behind Claire as she led them to the first stop: the drying house. They bunched up in front of Claire, giving her enough space to talk.

"And here is where the workers would prepare the tobacco to dry," Claire said.

A high school kid coughed audibly from somewhere in the back of the group.

"Do we have a question in the back?" Claire asked.

The teenager's braids swung beneath her beanie.

"You said *workers*," the teenager said. "Don't you mean *enslaved people*? It's not like these people had a choice. They were kidnapped from Africa, or from some other plantation down south."

The group began to rumble with chatter, agreeing with the vocal teenager's sentiments. Claire looked over her shoulder. The supervisor was often close by. But today, she saw him standing on the porch of the big house, talking with the chaperone. Old buddies from their college days, she assumed.

Then, Claire smirked. She looked at the script on her clipboard and flipped it around to show the students.

"You see this?" she said. "This is the script that I'm supposed to go by. Word for word."

She eyed the teenager. Her braids waved behind her as she rocked, daring Claire to go on.

"I'll give you a choice today. Do you want the scripted tour?" Claire asked. "Or do you want the *real* tour?"

"Give us the real story," the teenager said.

Claire smiled wider, a real smile. She was done holding back her thoughts. Done glossing over the true story. Done framing this place and this era as anything more than what it was. She was done staying silent. She was done sticking to the script.

The Game

It was all a performance. Always had been. The pre-game pep rally. The announcer over the crackling loudspeaker. The clever signs and the cheerleaders who shouted at fans that didn't need any more encouragement to yell. The runs up the middle. The deep passes. The hard-hitting tackles. The post-game helmet raises.

It was all a performance.

And Luke was the center of the whole show.

"Let's go, boys!" Luke shouted.

His team was huddled around him in the center of the field. The first quarter had just started. The ball was on the 20 yard line.

Luke's coach called an easy first play. Running back up the middle behind the fullback. Luke lined up behind the center.

"Down!" Luke bellowed.

His voice reached a bass octave that he had practiced over and over.

"Set!" he shouted.

He pushed his voice to reach an even more unnatural tone. He knew the audience loved it.

"Hike!"

The center snapped the ball to Luke. He stepped back and let the fullback pass him by and then he handed the ball to the running back. Automatic. The running back pushed through the line for a three-yard gain.

The offense jumped to attention again and circled around Luke. The noise of the crowd reverberated in his helmet, but he pushed himself to focus on his team.

"Break," the offense said, echoing in unison.

Luke lined up in the shotgun, a few strides behind the center. When he snapped the ball, Luke caught it and took a three-step drop. His offensive line smashed against the defense, creating a pocket of protection. Luke's eyes scanned downfield. His primary receiver was well-covered, so he looked to the next option: his second receiver streaking up the sideline.

Got him, Luke thought.

He cocked his arm back and launched the ball above the defense. It spiraled through the air. A beautiful ball. The receiver reached his arms out. He had nothing but green grass in front of him.

But he couldn't quite reach it. Luke had overthrown him by a few inches.

"Overthrown ball to a wide open receiver. Incomplete pass," the announcer said, his voice crackling over the loudspeaker.

Luke dropped his head. He knew the ball was overthrown. Looking through his facemask, his eyes drifted toward the stands. The crowd was shadowed behind the glare of stadium lights. He couldn't see his dad or his mom or his older brother, but he could feel their disappointment. They had trained all summer for big throws like this.

Luke's parents had high ambitions for him. They thought

that he had the potential to be a college quarterback at a major university. Maybe redshirt his freshman year. And the road to the college football stage needed to start with this season, his junior season. He needed to make big plays like the one he just failed to do.

Sometimes, he wished he was a simple member of the audience, a fan in the crowd whose only responsibility was to watch and cheer. He never got the chance to enjoy the game, to enjoy the performance. Sometimes, he wished he could kick his feet up on the bleachers and bask in the cool night air with a soda and his friends. No pressure to perform. No pressure to be perfect.

As he walked back to the huddle, Luke shook his helmet, partly to remove the doubt, partly to show the audience that he had remorse for his mistake.

It was all a performance, anyway.

"Let's run that same play again," Luke said to his team. "Brady, fake the inside route, and then go deep again. I got you."

He looked his second receiver straight in the eyes.

"On one."

"Break!" the team shouted.

Luke lined up in the shotgun again. The center snapped the ball. Luke dropped back. Quick, repetitive steps that he had rehearsed for years. He looked toward his first receiver and pump faked, setting the defense in place. And then, he looked across the field to Brady, whose defender had committed to the inside fake.

Brady is wide open, Luke thought. *No pressure. Easy throw.*

He gripped the ball near his ear and let it fly. Another perfect spiral sailed over the linebackers and hit Brady in the hands. He caught it in stride. And he kept striding. Right into the endzone.

The referee lifted both arms up. So did Luke.

"Touchdown!" the announcer shouted over the loudspeaker.

The crowd erupted. Stomps on the metal bleachers echoed across the field. Luke looked at the crowd. He was a part of their excitement. Yet, at the same time, he was separate from it. The focus of the group, but not a part of the group. Each person in the crowd was present, but anonymous. But Luke was on stage. They were in the audience. Sometimes, he just wanted to be a part of the crowd, to feel the weightlessness of anonymity.

But not today. Today, he was something else. Something elevated. He was the hero of the story.

It was all a performance, anyway.

The Coal Mine

Every kid in the neighborhood had heard the legends. The rumors. The folktales. Colby's older brother told him the stories. Colby's older brother heard the rumors from some older kids in the neighborhood. They heard it from their siblings, who heard from their parents.

That was the thing about legends; no one knew how long they'd been circulating.

One thing was certain: the folktales that surrounded the Dark Forest Mine had swirled for decades.

Ghosts had been spotted inside the mine shafts. Strange noises were heard after midnight along the railroad tracks that connected to the mine. A kid went into the mine and never returned. The mine was a direct portal to somewhere sinister.

Another thing about legends like these: they didn't scare kids away. They invited them in.

"You got your flashlight?" Colby asked.

"Sure do," Liz said. "Did you bring your knife?"

Colby reached into his backpack and showed her the pocketknife. Liz shook her head and smiled.

219

"I'm not sure what you're going to do with a knife against a ghost," Liz said. "But at least it'll help us against a monster."

Throwing his backpack over his shoulders, Colby began to walk. Liz grasped her backpack straps and followed. Darkness covered the interior of the forest, but the nearly full moon provided some light. Still, Colby and Liz used their flashlights to guide them.

"It's only a few more minutes down the path," Liz said. "That's what Shelly told me."

Colby stopped and looked at Liz, obviously annoyed.

"And what does Shelly know about the Dark Forest Mine?" he asked. "She's never been here."

Liz kept walking and passed Colby, who remained stationary until he realized that it was much darker without Liz's flashlight.

"No one really *knows* anything," Liz said. "Isn't that why we decided to go investigate the mine ourselves?"

"I guess you're right," Colby said. "Still, we should be ready for anything."

They didn't know much about the mine. But they did know some things for certain. The Dark Forest Mine used to produce most of the coal in the area. It was an active mine until about fifty years ago when the company shut it down and moved across the state. Aside from a few boards and a warning sign, the company left the mine intact. Eventually, it was absorbed by the forest.

And that's when the legends started.

Liz led the way, guided only by her flashlight. Leaves and sticks crunched beneath their feet. Slowly, their conversation faded, replaced by cautious awareness and darkness. They were getting closer.

And then they found it.

The entrance to the mine stood subtly, embedded into the side of the hill. Rotten wooden beams framed the entrance. An old etching read "Dark Forest Coal Mine" across the top, while a red-and-yellow warning sign that read "Warning: No Entry" stood in the dark portal.

Colby knelt down. Liz knelt by him. They shined their flashlights into the entrance tunnel, squinting their eyes to see farther.

"It's pitch black," Colby said. "Can't see a thing."

Liz shuddered.

"I guess we'll have to go inside," she said.

She stood and took a step forward toward the entrance. Hesitantly, Colby stood too. Looking at each other for reassurance, they both walked underneath the wood frame, around the warning sign, and into the mine.

Once inside, their flashlights proved more effective. They could see into the tunnel until it forked in two different directions.

"Imagine, a hundred years ago, all the miners that walked in here every day," Colby said.

"Yeah," Liz said. "And imagine all the ones that didn't make it out."

They had heard about the accidents. The cave-ins. The explosions. And they saw their neighbors, old guys from back then who had a hard time walking or breathing. Guys with missing fingers or busted eardrums. Those weren't legends.

Colby's flashlight drifted to the right, toward the earthen dirt wall. A quick flash caught his attention. His breath vacated his lungs and his heartbeat skyrocketed.

"Did you see that?" he whispered.

"See what?" Liz asked.

Nervously, Colby shined his flashlight back toward the wall. The same flash happened again.

"That," he whispered.

Liz looked at him and, even though he couldn't see her face, Liz raised an eyebrow.

"Your flashlight beam just reflected off an old lamp," Liz said.

She walked over to the wall and pointed to a fifty-year-old glass lamp case that still hung on the wall. Colby clutched his chest, forcing his breathing to return to a normal pace.

"You think that's the ghost that everyone says they saw?" Colby asked.

"Probably," Liz said. "I'll bet people see it and panic and run."

Liz chuckled. Colby forced himself to laugh. He allowed Liz to continue the walk down the tunnel, a tunnel that got darker and colder with each step.

"You think the people that owned this mine are still around?" Liz asked, trekking deeper into the tunnel.

"Probably not," Colby said. "But the company is still around. Still making money."

Even though the company had closed the Dark Forest Mine, they continued to buy up new mines throughout the mountains. It was one of the wealthiest companies in the state. Its CEOs always ran for big-name titles, like Governor and Senator.

The miners never ran for office.

"Did you hear that?" Liz asked.

A rustling noise echoed from somewhere near the entrance to the mine. From where they had just been. Colby snapped his head around and shined his flashlight toward the entrance. Liz stepped in front of him and shined her light as she crept toward the wooden frame.

The rustling grew louder.

And then, Liz turned around and laughed.

"It's a small tree branch blowing in the breeze," she said, pointing outside the tunnel.

Colby looked up and noticed the branch. And he noticed the sound. Wind blew into the tunnel and created a howling sensation. Shining his light back down the tunnel, he realized that nothing was coming after him. Nothing was there except vacant space. The resources had been extracted, burned in steam engines and factories, evaporated into the polluted air.

"There are no ghosts in here," Liz said. "It's just people getting jumpy and superstitious."

"Yeah," Colby said. "It was all in our heads."

"Oh well," Liz said. "At least we can say we did it."

Liz started to walk away from the mine, back into the darkness of the forest. Colby followed, leaving the ghosts to rest in the darkness of the mine.

The Speech

Wisconsin

The crowd packed the park in front of the makeshift stage. People seemed to form an endless mass, dissipating into the horizon, blending in with sunset behind them. There had to be thousands of people out there. And they were all silent.

Bryson stood backstage. Well, technically he was *side*stage. He could see the speaker at the podium and the crowd in front of the stage, but the crowd couldn't see him.

But they would soon enough.

The woman who spoke at the podium held a fancy title. Bryson wasn't exactly sure who she was, but he had heard someone call her "Senator" or something, so she must have carried some heir of importance.

The next spot at the podium belonged to Bryson.

"You ready, little man?" the event manager said.

It was the third time the event manager had called him that. And it was starting to get on Bryson's nerves.

"I guess," Bryson said. "There's a lot of people out there."

"There sure are," the event manager said. "That's what happens when your candidate has popular ideas."

* * *

A few weeks ago, the candidate's event manager contacted Bryson's mom. Somehow, they figured out her phone number. Political connections, Bryson guessed. They wanted Bryson to speak at the candidate's campaign event at the park.

Bryson didn't think much of it. He was Student Body President of his middle school, after all. It made sense that other politicians would reach out and try to connect.

"What's the theme of the speech?" Bryson asked.

"Respect," his mom said.

She looked sideways, and then returned her glare to Bryson.

"You know they're going to proofread and edit and change *anything* you might say that goes against their campaign," she said. "You can't just say what you want."

"Sure I can," Bryson said. "*They* asked *me* to speak. Not the other way around."

Bryson's mom raised an eyebrow.

"Just try to lay low," she said. "Not like your campaign speech for Student Body President."

Bryson fought the urge to laugh. He had called the school district superintendent's policies on the dress code "an antiquated piece of prejudicial horse manure." In front of the superintendent. The candidate's campaign manager must not have caught that one.

Two weeks before the campaign event, the campaign event manager showed up at Bryson's house with a pre-written speech. He sat in the living room while Bryson read it.

"What do you think?" the event manager asked.

"About what?" Bryson asked.

The event manager rolled his eyes.

"About that speech," he said. "That's the speech we're gonna make you...that we *suggest* you read."

Bryson tried to look impressed. Or at least look not insulted.

"It's interesting," Bryson said. "Thanks for the suggestions. I'll try to incorporate this into my original speech."

"You were planning on reading an *original* speech?" the event manager asked.

"Y'all asked me to give a speech," Bryson said. "So *I'm* going to give a speech."

The event manager placed his hands on his knees and elevated off the couch. He reached into his briefcase and removed a sheet of paper with bullet points.

"That's fine," the event manager said. "Here are the talking points that you need to address, then. And don't stray from these. We asked you to speak *for* us. And this is how you're going to do it."

Bryson plastered a fake smile on his face. He took the talking points and robotically shook the event manager's hand.

"I'll check in next week to review and finalize your prepared remarks," the event manager said.

Bryson waved to the event manager as he walked down the steps. As soon as he got in his car, Bryson threw away the pre-written comments.

Terrible, Bryson thought.

He reclined on the couch and read through the campaign's talking points. It stated ridiculous ideas like *America for Americans, law and order, help big businesses,* and *down with the welfare state.*

Bryson knew that these terms were code for something else. Something that put the interests of one group over the welfare of all people.

Grabbing his mom's phone, he called the event manager and told him that the idea of writing his own speech seemed too daunting after all. He would just use the pre-written speech instead.

Leaving the pre-written remarks in the trash can, he went to the desk in his room, pinned the vicious talking points to his bulletin board, and got to work.

* * *

The stage shook with the applause from the crowd. The famous politician onstage threw her hands in the air, triumphantly declaring a big win for the candidate. As the politician walked off the stage, the event manager clapped his hands together.

"You ready, little man?" he asked.

"Sure am," Bryson said.

He steeled his courage.

"Just stick to the script that we wrote for you and you're going to be fine," the event manager said.

"Don't worry," Bryson said. "I'm good."

Bryson heard his name called over the speaker system. Holding his script lightly, Bryson strolled onto the stage. The crowd erupted.

He stepped up to the podium and looked out at the sea of people. For a moment, he glanced back at the event manager, who returned the glance with a thumbs-up. From the front row of the crowd, Bryson's mom blew him a kiss. Bryson took a single, deep breath. And he bellowed into the microphone.

"Good evening, everyone," Bryson began. "My name is Bryson, and I'm the Student Body President at King Middle

School. I was asked to speak here tonight to talk about a single topic: respect."

The crowd cheered. Bryson paused to let the applause fade.

"I want a leader."

The crowd erupted. Bryson waited for the applause and the shouting to fade before he continued. They needed to hear this.

"I want a leader who exemplifies the quality of respect above almost any other quality," Bryson said. "I want a leader who leads by example, a leader who knows that they need to give respect in order to get it."

The crowd continued to cheer. Bryson eyed the event manager, who by now had noticed that this was not the pre-written script.

"We need a leader that shows respect to *all* people," Bryson continued. "Not just a select few. We need a leader who shows dignity to those with different ideologies, beliefs, and backgrounds, not just those who have received privilege since our country's inception. We need a leader who shows humanity to those who are struggling, not just those who have it easy. We need a leader who acknowledges the injustice that others face, even though he might not experience it himself. We need a leader who prioritizes the most vulnerable members of our society, not just those who inherited power in our society. We need a leader who understands that kindness is not a form of weakness, but the greatest form of strength."

Bryson paused. He heard one, singular applause coming from the front row. He saw his mother cheering wildly in an ocean of silence.

The event manager began to step subtly toward Bryson. But Bryson knew the event manager wouldn't risk making this a scene. So Bryson continued.

"We need a leader who is not afraid to do what is *right*," Bryson said, "not what his party and his super rich donors want him to do. We need a leader who will acknowledge how the successes and failures of our past have contributed to the successes and failures of our present. We need a leader who will place his people above his own self-image. We need a *real* leader!"

With that, he grabbed his script and strolled off the stage. The event manager tried to grab him by the elbow, but Bryson shrugged him off. Once they were finally out of the crowd's view, the event manager stepped to Bryson and crossed his arms.

"And what did you do that for?" the event manager asked.

Bryson smiled.

"You asked *me* to speak," Bryson said. "So I spoke."

The Land

Cole sat on his horse. A tumbleweed appeared from nowhere and blew across the dirt path before disappearing back into nowhere. The warmth of the day began to subside, shifting into an evening chill.

Adjusting his hat and pulling up his collar against his permanent five o'clock shadow, Cole encouraged his horse forward. The horse began a slow trot along the dirt.

"There we go, fella," Cole said.

Maybe he was speaking to the horse. Or maybe to himself. Rides like this used to be easy for Cole. He would never admit it out loud, but it hurt his joints if he rode too long anymore.

But it didn't matter. He didn't have many of these rides left.

Despite the difficulties, Cole needed the alone time to wander his land. He needed the time to clear his mind, to organize his thoughts. And talk to his horse.

The horse galloped along the grass until it came to a ridge that overlooked most of Cole's land. Small pockets of trees collected around rocky outcropping in the otherwise vast expanse of grassland. Two small creeks ran through the land, one on either side of the property. Enough water to sustain the cattle, but not enough to produce much agriculture.

Cole loved this land.

He remembered walking the property boundary as a kid, following his dad. The old man, gruff and grizzly, explained so many intricacies of the land and the cattle and the horses.

"See the direction the grass is blowing in the wind?" his dad asked. "Means there's cold weather coming in from the north. Time to move the cattle to the field by the cliffs and the trees so they have some protection from the weather."

But his dad passed away too soon. Cole had to learn a lot on his own.

This land had been his livelihood. And he treasured the earth and the water and the grass and the trees. It was his. But it also belonged to the past, and to the future. His ancestors hadn't earned the land. They stole it. Cole knew that. But he had it now. And it was his job to protect it.

And he knew that change was coming, forces that looked to take away the land's life. The signs were everywhere. New high-rise apartments and strip malls and more oil drilling. Less water in the streams. More severe winters. Every summer was warmer than the last.

Cole knew that he had to protect his land from these impending forces.

He hoped his son and granddaughter were up to the task. Not that he didn't believe in their capacity to foster the land. He had no doubt about their capabilities. It wasn't that at all.

But he did worry about the state of the country, the state of the world. It would make things so much harder for them.

"Things used to be so much easier," Cole muttered. "This land used to be so respected. So disconnected from what was going on anywhere else."

Cole remembered waking up and reading the newspaper at the kitchen table. The local stuff applied, but the national news seemed so removed, so inconsequential to his daily routine.

He remembered getting on his horse and moving the cattle from one grazing area to the next. Repairing fence posts. Meeting with restaurant owners and store managers to negotiate beef sales. Real, face-to-face conversations. Sometimes they talked about beef sales. Most of the time they didn't.

Sometimes, he'd go into town and buy a shirt, or some groceries. Buy them from an actual human being.

Sitting around the dinner table with his kids, young humans without phones, without constant connection to everyone else's collective minds, Cole remembered genuine conversation. They didn't always agree, but they connected.

"Yep," Cole said, "things sure used to be simpler. Things keep changing, and they're passing right by me."

He stopped the horse near a small rock cliff and stared. Not at anything in particular. But at everything all at once.

"Sunset looks pretty tonight," Cole said.

His horse nodded its head forward.

"I know you see it too," Cole said. "It's beautiful. All of it."

He looked toward the horizon. The sun was setting over his modest farmhouse. The house where he had learned from his parents, where he had raised his own kids, where he had learned to maintain balance on his land, learned to preserve it with integrity.

"And it will stay beautiful," he said. "No matter what changes."

Acknowledgments

First and foremost, I want to thank my family for giving me the inspiration and courage to find the value in the stories of everyone around me. Thank you for instilling the value of empathy within me, providing me with opportunities to learn from as many perspectives as I could.

To my wife: thank you for always pushing me to be a better version of myself. Thank you for giving me unconditional love and support as I bounce ideas back and forth. Thank you for giving me time to be creative. I love you.

To my children: thank you for providing my life with so much light and life. Seeing the world through your eyes is a privilege and an honor. You continue to teach me the value of empathy, the value of seeing the world through your eyes.

To my parents: thank you for establishing an appreciation for people, cultures, and experiences that aren't familiar to me. And thank you for continuously reminding me that my own story is also valuable. You've given me the strength I need to share stories, my own stories and those of other people.

To my teachers and mentors: thank you for cultivating my creativity and providing me with learning opportunities to hone the craft of the written word.

To my friends: thank you for adventuring with me. Thank you for always pushing me to expand my horizons and for diving into experiences that provide learning, growth, and self-improvement.

And to my ancestors: thank you for paving the way forward. Thank you for your wisdom, your mistakes, and your successes that set the path for me to follow. And thank you for being the whisper in my ear every single time I sit down to write.

About the Author

Tom Malone was born and raised in Portland, Oregon, where he learned to love rain, coffee, and books. He spent time exploring the city, the forest, and the coast. Malone studied journalism and history at the University of Oregon, Spanish at *la Universidad de Oviedo*, and earned his master's degree from the University of Portland.

He has taken dozens of road trips throughout the United States and continues to travel throughout the world. Currently, Malone teaches secondary English near Denver, Colorado, where he camps, fishes, hikes, and snowboards often.

Also by Tom Malone

Ghosts of Machu Picchu

Quinn has everything that he could ever want: a high-paying job, an adoring girlfriend, and an established life in the big city. Still, he feels a void in life that he can't seem to fill. And then, everything changes. Quinn finds himself alone in Peru, where he embarks on an adventure to trek to the legendary city of Machu Picchu. The journey, shrouded in mystery, will shape his life forever.

Captured

Michael had his entire future planned. He was going to propose to the love of his life and he had saved enough money to buy a house in the country. But, after a celebratory night out in the city, Michael wakes up in an underground tunnel system, the hidden network for the city's illicit activities. He's a prisoner, chained to a post. Captured. After a march through the underground tunnels, Michael is sold into servitude to a ship captain bound for Shanghai, destined for a life of misery, of invisibility, of disappearance. But, as Prohibition dawns in the United States, opportunities arise. Opportunities for gain, for loss, and for revenge.

Portlanders

Portland, Oregon: just another big American city. Tall buildings, millions of people, systemic problems, and a vibrant culture. In this collection of fictional short stories, take a walk through Portland from the perspectives of everyday people. Everybody experiences the city differently based on their own lenses, their own backgrounds, and their own motivations; it's the people who give a city its identity.

World History: A True Story

Explore the story of world history from its beginnings all the way to the modern day by looking at major civilizations, eras, people, and cultures that have shaped the world we live in. This brief overview of world history will spark interest, refresh learning, and provide a well-rounded look at how the world has reached its present state.

Across Americana

Ben's plan is unfolding perfectly. He is graduating from college. His dream job is set. Plus, his girlfriend is staying in his hometown and marriage is on the horizon. Then, on his college graduation day, he loses his job offer and his long-term girlfriend. Ben's best friend is leaving for the East Coast at sunrise. With nothing to hold Ben back, he embarks on a spontaneous cross-country road trip to New York City to begin an unforeseeable future. Along the journey, Ben encounters adventures that change his future forever.

Sloan Fitzpatrick: Middle School Journalist

Sloan Fitzpatrick is nervous about his first day of seventh grade. His best friend moved to another state. The school bully grew taller over the summer, while Sloan remained short. Plus, he registered for a Newspaper class just because his crush was the Editor-In-Chief, even though he knew nothing about journalism. After interviewing a city politician for his first assignment, Sloan finds himself wrapped up in the school newspaper. But he also finds himself caught in a political corruption investigation and he's in way over his head. Now, how's he supposed to handle seventh grade?

In the Shadow of the Spanish Sun

Jason embarks on a six-month journey to study abroad in Spain. When he arrives, he knows nothing but his own culture: an environment of greed, spiraling economic standards, and fast-paced rat races. After encounters with immigrant pick-up soccer, exotic cultures, and pushing the limit of fun, Jason dives too deep into these Spanish subcultures. He may find it difficult to return to his life in the United States. Then, he meets a girl. Will love turn him into an expatriate?